Danger: Dinosaurs!

A Science Fiction Novel

Danger: Dinosaurs!

By RICHARD MARSTEN

Jacket and Endpaper Designs
by Alex Schomburg

Cecile Matschat, Editor

Carl Carmer, Consulting Editor

THE JOHN C. WINSTON COMPANY
Philadelphia • Toronto

To SHIRLEY
my mother-in-law

Acknowledgments

My sincere thanks and appreciation to Dr. Frederick P. Young, the geologist who first introduced me to the Jurassic period, and who graciously and kindly checked the completed manuscript for technical accuracy.

R. M.

The Time Slip

Let us imagine an intricate combination of tubes and coils and relays and knobs and dials and knife switches. Let us suppose that the mind of man has so combined these unrelated pieces of machinery as to allow them to alter the steady progress of time.

Let us call this combination a Time Slip.

Let us assume that the Time Slip can take us back into the past. It can take us to yesterday. It can take us to last Christmas. It can take us back, back . . .

Back to look over the shoulder of Abraham Lincoln studying his books in the flickering light of a candle in a cabin long, long ago . . .

Back to Valley Forge, to stand beside General George Washington, to shiver beside the Continental Army, to watch the birth of a nation . . .

Back to Columbus, and the decks of a wooden ship

beneath his feet, and the sails of the Nina, the Pinta and the Santa Maria bright in the ocean sunlight . . .

And farther back . . .

Back to the Crusades, and back to Kublai Khan, and back to the days of the Egyptians . . .

Or why not, why not back to the very beginning? Why not back a million years, ten million years, a hundred million years?

The earth is new, rampant with life, alive with dinosaurs.

The Age of Reptiles.

This is where we will go in these pages. The Time Slip is ours to use as we will. Let us go back to the beginning.

R. M.

Contents

Chapter 1 Back a Hundred Million Years

THE sign was big and white and forbidding. It rose suddenly from the green grass surrounding it and jutted against the pale blue sky like the outstretched palm of a traffic policeman. Marching across the sign in bold black letters were the words:

TIME SLIP
AUTHORIZED PERSONS ONLY

Chuck Spencer looked at the sign and passed nervous fingers through his blond crew cut. His brother Owen had asked him to wait right on this spot, but that had been a full fifteen minutes ago and Chuck was beginning to worry a little.

He looked around nervously, saw the wide stretch of barbed-wire fence that enclosed the grassy area. The sky arced overhead like a giant blue parasol, sprinkled here and there with cottony wisps of clouds.

1

A mild breeze ran its fingers through the grass, setting the insects to buzzing gently.

It was a quiet scene, a landscape devoid of any tenseness. And yet, Chuck wanted to ram his knuckles against his mouth and bite on the flesh. He felt like jumping up and down or screaming or running from one end of the grass to the other.

He was being foolish, he knew. After all, Owen went on a slip almost every two weeks. It was a common occurrence for his brother like brushing his teeth or combing his hair. Just like that.

Well, it's not a common occurrence for me, he thought.

He unconsciously nodded his head in agreement with himself and turned to study the long, low building that squatted on the horizon. Owen had entered that building after leaving Chuck, and Chuck knew he was probably making last minute clearance checks, making sure that everything was set for the slip.

Chuck clenched his fists and thrust them deep into his pockets. *Stop being silly*, he told himself.

He glanced over his shoulder in anticipation. Where was everybody? What was keeping them?

Owen had given him careful instructions before he'd left.

"There's going to be a party of hunters here in about five minutes," he'd said. "They'll be looking for me, Chuck, and they're liable to get panicky if they don't find me. Just tell them you're my brother and that I'll be right back. I won't be a moment."

Well, he *had* been a moment. He had, in fact, been exactly seventeen moments and thirty-three seconds so far. And there was no sign of him yet.

Nor had the hunters arrived.

For a terrible moment, Chuck had the strange feeling that the Time Slip was already in operation. Maybe he'd already been whisked back a few years into the past and was waiting in vain for a brother who wouldn't appear for a good many months yet.

He was about to consider this seriously when he heard the sound of a motor in the distance. He turned suddenly, facing the large gate set in the barbed-wire fence. Two Security Policemen stepped from booths on either side of the gate, their rifles coming up automatically, as a jeep and a truck came into view over the rise of the hill. The truck raised a giant cloud of dust that smothered the jeep behind it. The vehicles moved closer to the gate, and Chuck heard one of the policemen shout, "Halt!"

The truck's brakes were jammed on suddenly, the wheels gripping the dirt road, spinning the rear end of the truck around to an abrupt stop.

From where he was standing, Chuck saw a big, barrel-chested man leap down from the cab of the truck. The man wore a pith helmet that shaded the strong, ruddy features of his face. He wore a white cotton shirt, open at the throat. Black, curling hair spilled from the throat of his shirt, ran down his muscular arms like short, dark weeds. He had dark brown eyes set on either side of a short, bulbous nose. His lips were thick, and his teeth were clamped tightly on the soggy end of a cigar.

"Where's the Time Slip?" the man shouted. His voice was gravelly, as if it had been tossed into a cement mixer and poured before it had mixed well. The voice grated on Chuck's nerves, made him wince slightly. He watched as one of the policemen walked closer to the big man.

"You're looking at it, Mister," the policeman said.

The man waved a hamlike hand at the grassy area behind the fence. "You mean that's it? Where's the machine? I don't see anything but grass."

"The controls are in the building up ahead," the policeman said.

The man nodded curtly and started back for the truck. He put one booted foot up on the running board and then turned his head. "Open the gate," he said. "We're coming through."

The other policeman spoke for the first time. He was bigger than the first and he carried his rifle with a lethal air of authority.

"Just a second, Mister," he said. "Let's see your papers."

"What?"

"Your papers. This ain't a ball park, Mister. This is a government project."

The big man took his foot off the running board and placed his hands on his hips. A broad smile covered his face, splitting it open in a gleaming burst of enamel. "Do tell," he said.

"You see that sign?" the policeman asked. He gestured with his head at the sign in front of which Chuck was standing.

"I see it," the big man said.

"Well, read it and weep. It says authorized persons only. If you're authorized, let me see your papers. If you're not you can turn those jalopies around and head for home."

The big man continued to smile as he moved closer

to the policeman. Chuck noticed, though, that he was smiling only with his mouth. His eyes were hard and unwinking.

"My name is Dirk Masterson," he said, the smile never leaving his face.

The policeman stared right back at him. "My name is Pat MacDougal. That still don't make you an authorized person, until I see your papers."

"Mr. MacDougal . . ."

"*Sergeant* MacDougal," the policeman corrected.

"Mr. MacDougal, perhaps you didn't understand me. I said my name was Dirk Masterson. This is my party, and we're scheduled to leave on a slip in about thirty minutes. I suggest you open your gate."

From behind the truck, obscured by the bulk of the larger vehicle, Chuck heard a man shouting, "Having trouble, Mr. Masterson?"

Masterson did not turn his head. "None at all, Brock," he called. To MacDougal, he said, "Open the gate, policeman."

Under the steady force of his gaze, the sergeant wavered slightly.

"How do I know you ain't a tempo?" he asked.

"A *what?*"

"A tempomaniac."

Masterson laughed, throwing his head back. "That's absurd," he said. "Open that gate at once."

"That gate stays closed until I see your papers," MacDougal said. "You can just pretend I'm St. Peter."

Masterson doubled his fists, and the muscles on his arms bulged with the effort. "Arthur!" he shouted.

Chuck saw the movement behind the windshield of the truck as the driver slid across the seat. He watched

as a tall Negro swung his legs over the side and leaped
down to the ground, a spurt of dust rising beneath his
heels.

"Yes, Mr. Masterson?" he asked.

He was bigger than Masterson, with broad shoulders
that tapered down to a narrow waist. He wore a white
T-shirt, and the color of his skin was soft against the
cotton. His head was compact, covered with close-cut
hair that fitted his skull like a cap. The features of his
face were classical, almost chiseled from black marble,
Chuck thought. He watched as the Negro began walking toward Masterson with purposeful strides.

"See what this idiot wants," Masterson snapped.

"Yes, sir," Arthur said. He reached into his back
pocket and pulled out a sheaf of papers which he
handed to MacDougal. "I imagine he's looking for
these," he said, his teeth flashing against his face.

"If you had papers, why didn't you show them in
the first place?" MacDougal complained. He took the
papers and examined them carefully while Arthur
waited. "These are fine," he said. "If you'll get back
in the truck, I'll open the gate."

"You'll be reported for this, you know," Masterson
said softly.

Arthur grinned, taking the papers back, and said,
"He was only doing his job, Mr. Master . . ."

"Nobody asked you," Masterson snapped.

The grin vanished from Arthur's face. For an instant
a hurt expression flickered in his eyes. And then it was
gone, replaced by the quiet planes of his emotionless
features. "Yes, sir," he said.

"Let's get back to the truck," Masterson said. He

turned to the guard once more and repeated, "You'll be reported for this."

MacDougal shrugged. "Go ahead, Mister, report me. My job is to stop tempos from scooting back into the past. As far as I'm concerned, everybody's a tempo until he proves himself otherwise." He shrugged again. "Go ahead. Report me."

"I will. I will, all right. Mistaking me for a tempomaniac. Of all the utter rot." He turned on his heel and strode for the truck, an indignant trail of dust rising behind him. Arthur walked to the other side of the truck and climbed in behind the wheel.

From the jeep, Chuck heard the same voice call, "Everything okay, Mr. Masterson?"

"We're rolling now," Masterson said, leaning out of the cab.

MacDougal walked into the guard booth and closed a switch. There was a gentle hum of machinery as the gate slid back.

The truck exploded into life, its motor roaring to the quiet countryside. Behind it, the jeep added its tiny voice to the general clamor. There was a grinding of gears as Arthur set the truck in motion. The big vehicle rumbled through the gate, followed by the jeep, and the gate slid shut behind it.

Chuck stepped away from the sign and waved his arm over his head. He kept waving as the vehicles moved closer. The truck shuddered to a halt some three feet from Chuck, and Masterson poked his head out of the cab.

"What is it now?" he said irritably. "Another 'Guardian of the Gates'?"

"I'm Chuck Spencer," Chuck said. "My brother is Owen Spencer, the guide for the expedition."

"Where is Owen?" Masterson wanted to know. "We had the devil's own time getting past that blockhead at the gate."

Chuck's glance wavered for an instant, his eyes meeting Arthur's behind the windshield. "He was only doing his job," Chuck said. "Tempos are more plentiful than you may realize."

Masterson shrugged this aside and shifted the cigar butt between his teeth. "Where's your brother?"

"He'll be here in a moment. He asked me to tell you to move your equipment close together. We'll be leaving shortly."

"You mean he wants the jeep alongside the truck?"

"Yes, I guess so."

Masterson jumped down from the cab and shouted, "Pull her up, Brock."

The jeep clashed gears and swerved away from the truck, moving back in a wide arc. The gears sounded again, and it pulled up alongside the truck. There were two men and a young girl in the front seat.

The man behind the wheel pulled up the emergency brake and hopped out of the small vehicle. "What was all the trouble back there?" he asked Masterson.

"A small man with a big gun," Masterson said bitterly. "Insisted on seeing our papers." He dismissed this with a wave of his large hand. "You know how petty a petty official can get, Brock."

The other man nodded. He was tall and thin and he wore black slacks, the cuffs shoved into the tops of his black boots. His shirt was gray, and his throat and face were a startling white against the darker colors. He had a long lantern jaw, a long nose and two glittering black eyes that darted nervously over Masterson's face. His eyebrows made a black gash across his forehead like a shaggy, elongated hyphen. He reminded Chuck of a vulture.

"Well," he said, "where's our guide?"

Chuck stepped forward and extended his hand. "My name is Chuck Spencer," he said. "My brother Owen will be guiding us."

The thin man took Chuck's hand, squeezed it faintly, and let it go instantly. "I'm Brock Gardel, Mr. Masterson's assistant."

Chuck nodded and was about to say something when Masterson said, "What's keeping your brother, son?"

"I don't know. I guess he . . ."

"Well, he'd darned well better hurry." Masterson glanced at his watch and then set his mouth into a tight line. He looked off toward the building on the horizon. "Is that him now?" he asked suddenly.

A figure had stepped out of the building and was heading for the group.

"That's Owen," Chuck said happily.

Owen waved, and Chuck waved back, watching his brother walk toward them with long strides. He was taller than Chuck, six-two to his brother's five-ten. He had Chuck's blond hair, but he wore it longer, and it fell across his forehead in unruly strands as he hurried across the grass.

When he was close enough, he called, "Hiya!"

"What kept you?" Masterson asked.

Owen sighed deeply. "Routine checkup. Always a pain in the neck." He rubbed his hand over Chuck's head. "Meet everyone?" he asked.

Chuck glanced quickly at the girl and the man still in the jeep. "Just about," he replied.

"Fine, fine," Owen said. He followed Chuck's eyes to the jeep, and noticed the girl for the first time. "Your niece," he said to Masterson, "is she coming along?"

"Why, yes," Masterson replied. "I thought you understood that from the beginning." He frowned slightly. "You don't have any objections to that, do you? I've got papers for her and everything."

"No objections at all," Owen said, smiling. "Except, well, the terrain where we're headed is a bit rugged, and I was . . ."

"Denise is a strong girl," Masterson said. "She'll make out fine."

"All right, if you say so."

Masterson looked at Chuck, then said, "I hadn't expected your younger brother to be with us."

Owen grinned. "I wangled permission from the government. On the records, he's my assistant." Owen noticed the look that crossed Masterson's face and he hastily added, "I think Chuck can prove mighty helpful on a hunt. This is his first time slip, but he knows prehistoric animals the way he knows house pets."

Gardel lifted his brows incredulously. "Really?"

"I just know a few," Chuck murmured.

Owen laughed. "A few, huh? He can name every beast that ever walked the earth." He paused and then said, "And he could probably draw pictures of most of them."

"Gee, Owen," Chuck said, "I'm not really that . . ."

"When do we leave?" Masterson asked suddenly.

Owen looked at his watch. "In about fourteen minutes. If you'll gather your party, I'd like to go over a few rules."

"Get every one together, Brock," Masterson said.

Gardel waved to the man in the truck. "Pete, come on over." He nodded his head at the girl. "Denise, you too." He turned to Owen and explained, "Pete's our cook."

Chuck had a good opportunity to study the cook and Masterson's niece as they walked over from the jeep. Together, they formed a blazing riot of color.

Denise had glistening blonde hair that caught the rays of the sun and sent them shimmering across the field.

Pete, walking alongside her, had a fiery crown of red hair capping his skull. He was a corpulent little man, waddling next to Denise like a pet duck. His green eyes were sparkling and seemed to shower his face with thousands of freckles that fell helter-skelter on his skin.

Denise, on the other hand, was tall and slim, her hair clipped short on her neck, her eyes as brown as the earth. She smiled happily as she made herself comfortable in the tight circle.

"I'll just give you the rules and the reasons for them," Owen said simply. "We're not here to argue them. These are all government regulations, and I have the authority to place under arrest any person violating them during the slip. Is that clear?"

Owen took the silence for assent, cleared his throat and went on.

"To begin with, no one is to shoot with anything

but a camera when we get to the past. That's the rule;
the reason for it is simple. If hunters were allowed to
kill off animals at random, we'd likely find a present-
day species wiped out because we'd killed off all its
ancestors. Remember that the present is built upon the
past. Any change in the past will necessarily affect the
present. Therefore, no shooting. Just cameras." He
smiled and added, "And I hope you're bringing plenty
of film."

"Go on," Masterson said, "let's get on with this."

"Second, no one will go within three feet of the
force field."

"What's that?" Gardel asked.

"A field of energy enclosing a mile-square area. The
invisible wall generated will keep the animals out and
us in. I don't want to chance any short circuit, however, so no one will go any closer than three feet from
it. That's the second rule."

"This sounds like a school for bad boys," Masterson
said. "You'd hardly think I was paying—and heavily,
I might add—for the privilege of going back into the
past."

Owen grinned. "I'm sorry, but the rules must be
obeyed."

"All right, what's your next edict?" Masterson asked.

"Simply this. I give all the orders on this slip, and
the orders will be obeyed. That's all."

"That's enough," Masterson said, a slight smile on
his lips.

"Does everyone understand?" Owen asked. A chorus
of yeses greeted his question. "Fine." He looked at his
watch again. "We'd better get into the trucks and get
ready for the slip," he said. "The process is all auto-

matic, you know. We'll have to move the stuff up a little."

"Where to?" Arthur asked.

"See those white blocks set into the ground up ahead? Just drive up until your wheels touch them."

Arthur started the truck, with Owen clinging to the running board outside the cab. Owen waved back and shouted, "Bring the jeep up alongside it."

The truck stopped with its front wheels against the blocks. Gardel hopped into the jeep and brought that up, too. It stopped alongside the truck, looking like a sparrow perched near a mountain.

Owen looked at his watch again.

"We've got about four minutes. See those four red blocks in the ground?" He pointed to four large wooden blocks sunk into the ground to form the corners of a large square. "If we'll just keep inside those while the Slip is in operation, we'll all be fine." He paused and looked at his watch again. "Any questions?"

"Plenty," Masterson said. "How does the Time Slip work?"

Owen laughed a little and answered, "Everyone asks that. Truthfully, I don't know."

"You don't know?"

"Don't misunderstand me. I have some idea of the principle behind the operation, but I certainly don't know what makes that enormous machine tick. As a matter of fact, I don't think any one man knows."

"What's the principle, then?" Masterson asked.

"Well, we've got to picture time as . . ." Owen scratched his head. "Now, let me see. How can I best explain this to you?"

He thought for a few seconds, and then said, "Well, picture time as a phonograph record. Circular, with grooves cut into the wax. You place your needle in the outermost groove and it works its way toward the center of the record. The picture clear?"

"Yeah," Gardel said dubiously.

"All right, just take it a step further. Assume that the outermost groove of the record is the past. And the groove nearest the center is the present. When you play the record, the needle travels from past to present, right?" Owen glanced at his watch again. "I'd better hurry. We'll be slipping soon."

"I still don't get it," Masterson said.

"The point is simple. Most people erroneously feel that the past is dead and gone. But if we compare time to the record, we can see that the past is always there, coexistent with the present. For example, when we play the record, the first few bars of the song are over and done with as soon as the first groove is passed. But they are not dead and gone. All we have to do is move the needle back to the first groove and we'll get the first few bars of the song all over again."

"You trying to say that the past is going on right now, at the same time as the present?" Gardel asked.

"Exactly. All the Time Slip does is to move that needle, in effect. In other words, it slips the needle over the record, back from the innermost groove which is the present, to the outermost groove which is the past."

"How?"

"By shocking us back mostly," Owen replied.

"What? What'd you say?"

"When you're playing your phonograph, a sharp

bump will cause the needle to slip over the record. Same principle here. We'll be getting a series of sharp bumps, so sharp and so fast that we won't even feel them. Each bump will actually suspend us in time, like the needle popping into the air over the record. Each time we come down, we'll be slightly farther back in the past." Owen looked at his watch again and said, "We'll be going in about ten seconds. I'll have to cut this short, I'm afraid." A serious look crossed Owen's face, and he kept his eyes glued to the moving sweep hand of his watch.

"Nine seconds," he said. "Stand by."

Chuck felt a tight hand clutch his throat. Up until now, he had succeeded in keeping a firm grip on his emotions. But now they were ready to go! All the way back, far back into the past, back to the dim beginnings.

"Eight seconds."

His heart began to beat a little faster. He took his lower lip between his teeth, biting on it hard. He stared out at the grass, wondering what it would change to, wondering . . .

"Six, five . . ."

"Who's handling all this?" Masterson asked.

"The control room," Chuck blurted, surprised he could speak at all.

"Three, two . . ."

"God be with us," Arthur whispered gently.

"One!"

Chapter 2 Through the Force Field

CHUCK thought it was the beating of his own heart at first. All sound seemed to have stopped suddenly, the crickets, the faraway throb of an airplane motor, the shrill wail of a train whistle cutting across the afternoon. And then, quite abruptly, sound filtered back, but it came in waves—short, beating waves that rose and fell. Accompanying the sound was a faint flicker of light, on and off, on and off.

Chuck stood stockstill, not daring to move, hardly daring to breathe. The waves of sound assailed his ears in unintelligible succession. The area around the marked square was no longer visible through the flickering light. Chuck knew that each light-flick was actually part of the "bumping" process Owen had told them about earlier. And each "bump" was carrying them back farther into the past. A dancing array of colors greeted the eye, now green, now red, now a deep blue. Once or twice, Chuck thought he could distinguish shifting shapes in the flickering light. The colors swirled and danced, massing into a brilliant white, changing to gray, black, orange, yellow, one color blending with the next as they sped back over the years.

He felt no different than he had ten minutes ago. He was, in a small way, disappointed. He had expected something more glamorous, more dramatic. A giant machine, perhaps, with dials and gadgets and knife switches. A scientist in a white robe with a steaming flask in his fist. And the crackle of lightning from one terminal to another, the blue tingle of electricity. He had visualized an enormous screen upon which the colorful panorama of the past would parade. There he would see the Crusades or Columbus crossing the ocean with his small ships or the War Between the States or any and all of the wonderful things he'd only read about. Then the great dials would stop twirling, and the machine would cease its endless hum. He would open the knife switches, press the button which swung wide the glass doors of the big machine and step out into the past.

Instead, there was only the riot of colors and the confusing jumble of sound that beat against his ears.

Even that ended.

Quite abruptly, the sound vanished, and the colors evaporated. Chuck blinked his eyes and stared around him. The low, well-cropped grass of the Time Slip was gone. The white markers were gone. The four red blocks that had been set in the ground had disappeared. The building housing the intricate mechanism of the control unit wasn't on the horizon any more.

The land was alien, lushly green, steam rising from

the vegetation that covered the earth like a green carpet.

"This is it," Owen said softly. "We are now in the Jurassic period of the Mesozoic Era, approximately 100 million years back in time."

The party seemed stunned. They looked around them and said nothing. Gardel was the first to speak.

"What's that Jurassic and Meso . . . Meso *what?*"

"Mesozoic. Both are geologic terms. Mesozoic means 'intermediate life.' The geologists called this era that because of the development of so many life forms during this time."

"And Jurassic?"

Owen smiled. "That's one of the periods of the Mesozoic Era. It got its name from the Jura Mountains between France and Switzerland, where a great many rocks of this time were well exhibited and widely studied." Owen snapped his fingers. "We'd better get the force field in operation at once. They don't call this the Age of Reptiles for nothing." Quickly Owen swung his pack off his shoulders and dropped it to the ground. He unscrewed two screws at the top of the front panel, then lowered the front to reveal a many-dialed face. Several buttons were set in the face of the instrument, too, and Owen stabbed at two of them and began twisting one of the dials very slowly.

"The energy is now going straight up and around us," he explained, "like an umbrella. As soon as it clears the party . . ." He studied a meter that measured feet and then said, "There, that's it."

His hand flicked another dial and he began turning that, more rapidly this time. "I've dropped the field to the ground now and I'm moving it away from us gradually. It will force back any animal it encounters as it moves along. I'll keep it going until it stretches around us for a radius of one mile. That'll give us plenty of room to roam around in."

"Sort of like an invisible, upside-down fishbowl," Arthur said.

"Yes, that's it exactly," Owen replied, nodding his head and watching the footage meter. "Or a canopy of pure energy—electrically generated, of course."

"How do you know there'll be no animals left inside the field?" Masterson asked.

"I dropped the force field to the ground as soon as it cleared the party," Owen said, still watching the meter. "We're the only animals standing right here, as you can see." He grinned. "The electric charge will send anything else it hits running like the devil. You can rest assured the area will be cleared." He looked at the meter again and pressed another button on the face of the panel. "That does it. We can break ranks now."

All at once they seemed to realize where they were. They stared around in mute fascination, their eyes hungry for details.

Here was the beginning. Here was the earth in its comparative infancy, a wilderness of strange trees and rocks, a land as alien as the most distant planet.

Chuck swallowed hard, and his eyes roamed the land. Ferns covered the ground everywhere, steamy layers of mist rising from them like trails of smoke. The land was silent, slanted with dark gray slates, high outcroppings of sandstone and limestone, conglomerate, shale. Far in the distance, moving among the high plants like shadowy blurs, Chuck could see the bulky forms of animals roaming the edge of the force field. A shiver of apprehension tickled his spine.

Huge cycads, palmlike in appearance, with short stout trunks and clusters of long fronds, rose from the ground. He was surprised to see pine trees and evergreens jutting out of the rolling countryside. And here and there, like splashes of color on a monotonous green canvas, he saw a few flowering plants. These, he knew, were the great-great-grandfathers of the angiosperms, the seed-bearing, true flowering plants that constituted nine-tenths of the land plants in his own time.

The air was mild and it smelled of growing things, of the fetid odor of primitive growth run amok. The odor assailed the nostrils with almost physical force, crowded the senses, made them shrink back in revulsion. A moisture clung to the air like the heavy, water-filled denseness that precedes a summer storm. The sun was shining, though, bearing down with heavy golden rays that touched the plants and the ground with long fingers.

Spread among the pines and cycads and evergreens, their fan-shaped leaves reaching out to the sun, Chuck recognized the ginkgo or maidenhair trees with their fleshy fruit and edible nuts.

His eyes took all this in, and he was filled with a deep sense of wonder and awe. He knew, though, that this was merely the stage. The actors were still in the wings, waiting to put in an appearance. The blurred shadows he had seen on the edge of the force field, the bulky, ponderous, slow-moving shapes—these were what made Jurassic times. The reptiles.

He looked at the plants again and tried to visualize a stegosaur nibbling on the foliage, or a sauropod trampling over leaves, its long neck bobbing. He did not succeed. To him, the creatures were still something out of the imagination, something the scientists had thrown together from a few theories and a few old bones. He knew all the names, yes, and he had a mental picture of each of the beasts—but that was as far as it went. Unconsciously, his mind drew a line between fancy and reality. The bones, the books, the theories were all part of reality. The restored figures of the giant reptiles were still fancy to Chuck. They would remain fancy until he had seen them.

Somehow, he did not look forward to it. He had cherished the fantasy of the monsters, carried it in a secret pocket of his mind, the way he had carried a toad to school every day when he was twelve years old. He had the uneasy feeling that the theories would all be proved wrong, that the monsters would turn out to be tiny lizards instead of gigantic beasts. He did not want the dream to be shattered and he was not overly eager to put the theories to the test.

"What's so terribly special about this?" Masterson asked, breaking the silence. "This could be Africa or any other wilderness."

"It could be," Owen said softly, "but it isn't. This is America, Mr. Masterson. America many, many years before the first man put in his appearance."

"That's what I'd like to see," Pete said, his green eyes twinkling. "A real cave man."

"You'll find no men in Jurassic times," Owen said.

"As fas as we can tell, the first man appeared in the Cenozoic, about 99 million years from now."

"Cenozoic? What's that mean?" Gardel asked.

"It means 'Recent Life.' In our own time, Man was only one million years old, you must remember. But we're not in our own time any more. It'll be a long, long while before Man shows up."

"We should have gone to the Cenozoic, then," Masterson said. "I'd have liked to see a cave man, too."

"Time slips to any time inhabited by Man are forbidden by law," Owen said simply.

"That's a shame," Arthur said, shaking his massive head. "Primitive man must have been interesting."

"Please keep quiet, Arthur," Masterson said.

The flicker of anger sparked again in Arthur's eyes. He seemed about to speak, then he turned his head away. But not before Chuck had seen the hurt look settle on his dark features. Chuck turned to Masterson, anxious to learn what had provoked the sudden attack on the Negro. Masterson's eyes were blank. He had already forgotten what he'd said.

He pointed off to the dim figures in the distance. "Are those our game?" he asked.

"Yes," Owen said, his voice a little brisk. Chuck knew that his brother had heard Masterson's slur, too. Owen hadn't liked it either.

"Well," Masterson said, "this is supposed to be a hunt, so let's get started. This time is costing me a pile of money."

"It's for a good cause, Mr. Masterson," Owen said.

"Really? What cause is that?"

"The funds we collect from private hunting expeditions enable us to finance scientific expeditions. We've learned an awful lot about the past by . . ."

"Yeah, well let's go take a look at those animals," Masterson interrupted.

He strode over to the jeep and climbed in behind the wheel.

"Before we move from this spot," Owen said, "we'd better mark it. Did you bring the paint I asked for?"

"Sure," Masterson said, twisting the ignition key. "It's in the truck." Owen walked over to the truck, lifted the flap, and began rummaging around.

"Right near the tailgate," Masterson said quickly. "Don't go upsetting everything."

"I've got it," Owen called. He pulled his head from the canvas covering, emerging with a can of white paint and a brush. He pried the lid off the can, dipped the brush into the paint and began painting a large white square on the ground. "This will mark our spot," he said. He looked at his watch. "We've been here about ten minutes now, which puts our time of arrival at about two P.M. We've got to be back in this same spot one week from today at exactly that time. They'll slip us forward to the present, then."

"To the present?" Gardel asked.

"Well, to the future, really. I meant, to the present we were accustomed to."

"Come on," Masterson said. "Let's get rolling." He started the jeep, gunned it forward. "You can follow in the truck. I'm anxious for a look."

The jeep leaped forward like a runaway stallion, Masterson behind the wheel, his pith helmet pushed

back on his head. The jeep bounced over a jutting
rock, sprang high into the air and came down on two
tires, almost overturning. Masterson grinned, turned
the wheel sharply to avoid a low stump, and stepped
on the gas again.

Chuck saw Owen's brows curl onto his forehead,
watched a troubled look creep into his brother's eyes.

"What's the matter, Owen?" he asked.

"I don't like the way he's driving. This is rough
country, Chuck. I don't want any accidents." He
paused, turned and started walking toward the truck.
"We'd better go after him."

He hopped into the cab of the truck, and Chuck
climbed in after him.

"We'll be right back," Owen called. "Please feel
free to wander around at will."

He turned on the ignition key, started the truck
and gnashed the gears into place. He set the big
vehicle into motion, watching the small jeep up ahead.

"He's going like crazy!" Chuck said in surprise.

"I don't get it," Owen replied. "Where does he
think he's . . ."

"The force field!" Chuck shouted. "Suppose he . . ."

"Great jumping . . ." Owen never finished what
he was saying. His hands tightened on the wheel and
he pushed his foot down on the gas pedal. Chuck
watched the foliage sweep by in a green blur, large
palmlike leaves slapping the windshield as the truck
shoved its way over the rough terrain. The truck
rocked from side to side as it rolled over rocks and
stumps, dropped into deep ruts, its thick tires fighting ground for every inch. Up ahead, the jeep bounced

and rolled like a cork in an angry sea. Masterson was
clinging to the wheel as if it were a life preserver.

"Yell to him," Owen said anxiously. "Tell him he's
getting too close to the force field."

Chuck climbed out of the cab onto the running
board, clinging to the open door. He ducked as they
barged through the leaves that hung from a huge tree.

"Mr. Masterson!" he shouted.

His voice lifted over the roar of the truck motor,
fled into the foliage and echoed from the rocks.

"Mr. Masterson! The force field! You're heading
right for it!"

Masterson didn't seem to hear. He kept the jeep
going at its frantic pace, hopping over the ground like
a huge bullfrog.

"For Pete's sake," Owen said, "stop him, Chuck!"

"Mr. Masterson!" Chuck bellowed, holding to the
doorframe as the truck sped over the ground. "Stop!
The force field!"

Masterson turned his head and seemed to understand. He stood up like a man who'd been stuck with
a pin and suddenly leaped out of the jeep, hitting the
lush growth underfoot and rolling over into a ball.

The jeep plunged ahead recklessly, bouncing over
the ground in wild abandon.

"The jeep," Owen said. "It's going to crash the force
field, Chuck."

The jeep hurtled over a high, flat rock that jutted
into the air at a sloping angle. It cleared the end of the
rock like a diver leaving a diving board, hung on the
air for a moment and then fell earthward.

"Chuck!" Owen shouted.

There was a sudden crackling of electricity. The
jeep shuddered in a shower of sparks that surrounded
it for several moments like a shimmering halo. It
plunged ahead for several feet, carried by the force
of its momentum, and then it stopped dead in a flat
clearing of ferns.

"That does it," Owen said disgustedly.

"What, Owen?"

"Those sparks, didn't you see them? The jeep hit
our force field, and the metal shorted it. This is great,
positively great!"

"Wh—what are we going to do?" Chuck asked.

"I don't know. Pick up that egg-headed idiot first,
I guess. Of all the fool stunts." Owen's face was a
bright red. He kept his lips pressed tightly together
as he steered the truck to where Masterson was sitting on the ground, his elbows resting on his knees.

Owen stopped the truck beside him and leaned
out of the cab.

"Remember those orders I gave before we left?"
he asked, his voice fighting against the rage inside
him.

"I remember," Masterson said calmly.

"I said no one was allowed within three feet of the
force field. Do you remember that?"

"I'm . . . I'm sorry," Masterson said, lowering his
head. "I wanted to get out of the jeep before we hit.
I . . ."

Owen opened the door and dropped out of the
cab.

"Why were you driving like a madman in the first
place?" he wanted to know.

"I just . . . I was just anxious to see the animals

up close, that's all. I just wanted to take a good look
at them."

Owen nodded his head bitterly. "I'll let you in on
a secret, Mr. Masterson."

Masterson lifted his head hopefully. "What's that,
Owen?"

"You're *really* going to get a good look at the animals. You're going to be able to look down their
throats clear into their bellies!"

"Wh—what do you mean?"

"I mean you've shorted our force field. You've
effectively knocked down the only protection that
stood between us and the beasts out there. Do you
understand that, Mr. Masterson? Do you understand
what I'm trying to tell you?"

"You mean . . ."

"I mean there's nothing between us and the enormous reptiles that roam Jurassic times, that's what I
mean. Nothing, Mr. Masterson." He turned away in
disgust. "Get into the truck," he said harshly. "We'd
better get back to the party while we're still able to."

They climbed into the truck, Owen still sullen,
Masterson looking quite calm after what he'd done.
Owen started the motor without saying another word.

"What about the jeep?" Chuck asked.

Owen signed deeply. "It's probably still operable,
Chuck. You drive it back, will you?"

Chuck nodded and hopped out of the truck, walking quickly to the jeep. He stared around him uneasily, not at all content with their present position
now that the force field had been destroyed. He
climbed into the driver's seat and started the small
vehicle. "Okay," he called to Owen.

Owen swung the truck around, backing it over an outcropping of conglomerate. Then, straightening his wheels, he headed for the party in the distance.

Chuck glanced around him nervously as he drove the jeep forward. He thought of the restorations he'd seen of reptiles from this period, and a shudder worked its way up his spine.

Unconsciously, he stepped on the accelerator a little harder.

Chapter 3 Mutiny!

THE party surrounded Owen silently, listening to what he had to say. Masterson sat in the cab of the truck, his face void of any guilt. Denise dangled her feet over the tailgate and listened to Owen with her lower lip caught between her teeth. Gardel leaned against the fender of the jeep, his long body bent forward at a curious angle. Arthur squatted on the ground, turning a large fern over in his brown hands. Pete, his green eyes pensive, listened with interest.

"Our generator is useless now," Owen said. Chuck nodded silently, standing near his brother and looking at the thoughtful faces in the circle. "The force field is broken, and we've no way of putting up a new one."

"That's not so good," Pete said with a shake of his head. His red hair gleamed brightly in the sun, and there was a worried look on his face.

"It means there's nothing to keep the animals out

any more," Owen said. He clenched his fists, then
unclenched them quickly. "If there were some way
for us to get back to the present immediately, I
wouldn't hesitate a moment. Unfortunately, we'll
have to wait until the automatic process begins again,
one week from now."

Arthur sighed deeply. "That's a long time. Especially with all those animals out there."

"You're all behaving like a bunch of frightened
children," Masterson said suddenly. "What's there to
worry about? I understand these dinosaurs have
brains the size of peas. Surely, we can outsmart such
a stupid lot for a week."

"You may be able to outsmart them," Owen said,
"but do you think you can outrun them?"

"What? I don't understand you."

"I've seen these big babies in action, Mr Masterson.
Many of them are extremely ponderous and slow-
moving. But there are many others whose speed would
amaze you. I hope you never have to run a race with
Allosaurus, for example."

"Who?"

"*Allosaurus*," Chuck said, thinking of the beast,
forming a mental picture in his mind. "He was one of
the fiercest reptiles in Jurassic times, forerunner of
the largest flesh-eating animal ever to roam the earth:
Tyrannosaurus rex. Luckily, *Tyrannosaurus* doesn't
appear until later in geologic time."

"*Allosaurus* doesn't scare me," Masterson said, waving his hand in a palm-down gesture. "I've hunted
everything from elephants to rhinoceroses."

Owen grinned wryly. "I think you'll find Allosaurus
to be a little different from either of those animals."

"We're wasting time talking," Masterson said. "So I happened to short the force field. All right, so what?"

"I don't think you realize the seriousness of our position, Mr. Masterson. These animals . . ."

"These animals are only animals!" Masterson said forcefully. "They happen to be big, that's all."

"The bigger they come, the harder they fall," Gardel put in.

"Exactly. I don't see what everyone is making an issue about."

"No issue at all," Owen said tightly. "From here on in, I'm giving the orders, and they'll be obeyed. As far as I'm concerned, the hunting part of this expedition ended the minute we shorted the force field."

"What!"

"You heard me, Mr. Masterson. No one is to leave the vicinity of the trucks, starting right now. Is that clear?"

"This is absurd," Masterson complained. "I paid a handsome fee for the privilege of . . ."

"That has nothing to do with it!" Owen snapped.

Masterson leaned out of the cab, his face ruddy with rage. "It has a lot to do with it," he said. "I paid for a hunting expedition and, by Jupiter, I'm going to get one." He hopped out of the cab, angrily pushing aside a tall fern that blocked his path. Without looking back, he walked purposefully to the rear of the truck.

"Where are you going?" Owen asked.

Masterson's voice was low when he answered. "There's something I want to show you," he said.

He leaned over Denise sitting on the tailgate and

began rummaging around among the supplies
stacked in the back of the truck. After a few minutes'
search, he seemed to find what he was looking for.

"What do you want to show me?" Owen asked. "If
it's . . ."

"This!" Masterson said suddenly. He whirled from
the truck, a high-powered hunting rifle with a telescopic sight clutched tightly in his fists.

Owen looked at the gun and then raised his eyes
to meet Masterson's. "What is this?" he said.

"What does it look like?"

"You tell me," Owen said.

"I'll be happy to. It's as simple as it looks, my
friend. I paid an awful lot of money for this expedition. I'm also taking time off from my business to be
here. That's costing me additional money. I came here
to hunt and I was willing to go along with your 'cameras only' edict. That was before the force field col-
lapsed. Now, I think I need bigger protection than a
camera. You'll notice I came prepared for any even-
tuality."

"You'd better put that gun away," Owen said
softly. "No one's doing any hunting on this trip—
least of all with a gun!"

"That's where you're wrong," Masterson answered.
"Gardel, get another rifle from the truck."

Gardel didn't answer. He shoved himself off the
fender of the jeep and walked quickly to the rear end
of the truck. Denise watched him as he dug beneath
the supplies and slid out another rifle. Her eyes were
large with fright. Chuck looked at the rifles and then
tried to read Masterson's face. It was expressionless.
"Let's look at it this way," Masterson said, a smile

beginning on his face. "I paid for a hunting expedition. If I don't get what I paid for, I'm being cheated. A man has a right to protect his own investment. Isn't that true?"

"No, it's wrong. You're here by government permission. And law forbids the use of . . ."

"Oh, for Pete's sake, grow up!" Masterson snapped. "We're here to hunt—and we're *going* to hunt. Only we're going to do it the way we should, with guns. I'm going to bring back some real specimens for the museums, my friend. Specimens they can stuff in place of those reconstructed fossils they're using now."

"Forget this, Mr. Masterson," Owen said, trying to keep his voice down. "It'll only lead to trouble. If not now, then when we get back and I report this."

"We'll worry about that when the time comes," Gardel said.

"Yes," Masterson agreed. "Brock is right. We'll cross our bridges when we come to them. Right now, our first bridge is a little matter of dinosaur hunting."

Arthur suddenly got to his feet, shaking his head. "I don't like this," he said in his deep voice. "I don't like it one bit."

Masterson let out a sigh of exasperation. "Primitive times seem to have struck a responsive chord in your breast," he said. "I'd like to remind you who pays your salary, Arthur."

Arthur opened his mouth as if to speak and then changed his mind.

Masterson, content with his minor victory, said, "You'll drive Owen and his brother in the jeep, Arthur. Denise, Pete, Brock and I will lead in the truck."

"Nobody's going anywhere," Owen said firmly.

"Aren't you being a little ridiculous?" Masterson asked. "How can you stand there and argue with a man holding a gun? This gun could put a six-inch hole in an elephant, Owen."

"It's lucky I'm not an elephant, then," Owen said sourly.

"I imagine it could blow a man's head clear off," Masterson continued. "I'd hate to have to do that."

Owen began laughing loudly, and Chuck almost joined him until he remembered the seriousness of the situation.

"Stop behaving like a movie gangster," Owen said. "It doesn't fit well with your executive's personality."

Masterson smiled. "No, Owen, not a gangster. A hunter. And a hunter shoots to kill." He flicked his thumb against the safety catch above the trigger. "Shall we get started now?"

Chuck stared at Masterson incredulously and then said, "Why, I think he means it, Owen."

Owen was equally surprised "Yes. Yes, I really believe he does. I really believe so."

"That's absolutely right, Owen," Masterson said. "I do not intend to sit here and wait for those slow-witted dinosaurs to come and find me. I've got a gun and ammunition and I'm going to do a little hunting. Now get into the jeep, both of you."

Chuck hesitated, looking to his brother for a decision.

Owen shrugged. "Sure. We have no choice. We'll go along. But only so I can keep an eye on you. You're still my responsibility, Mr. Masterson."

"Thank you. I appreciate your concern."

Owen turned his back to Masterson and began

walking to the jeep. Arthur was already behind the
wheel, his face emotionless, his eyes staring straight
ahead at the shadows moving in the distance.

"Denise," Masterson said. "You'll come up in the cab
with Brock and me. Pete, you'll ride in the back.
Let's get rolling." He lifted his niece down from the
tailgate and popped her into the cab. Gardel started
the engine as Masterson swung aboard.

In the jeep, Arthur twisted the ignition key and
muttered, "I don't like this at all."

The truck moved ahead over the lush growth,
flattening ferns and bushes, its tires skidding over
wet rocks. In the smaller vehicle Chuck peered
through the windshield and then turned to Owen.

"What are we going to do?"

"What *can* we do? They've got guns."

"Do you really believe they'd use them on us?"

"I don't know, Chuck. This is the first time anything
like this has ever happened to me. Masterson is acting
like a madman. If we're not careful, he'll get us all
killed out here."

Arthur said nothing. He kept his hands tight on the
wheel and his eyes glued to the treacherous ground
ahead.

They moved forward slowly, like children taking
their first steps. The truck hugged the deeply vegeta-
tive ground, rumbling noisily to the ferns and cycads.
Behind the truck, the jeep obediently shoved its way
through the thick greenery that clung tenaciously to
the land.

The shrubbery parted reluctantly. It was like a
sentient thing forbidding passage. It clawed at the
fenders, slapped against the metallic sides, stuck out

long, jutting roots to ensnare the tires. Insects flurried
into the air in frightened hordes as the vehicles pushed
their way deeper into the lush plants. Chuck was
surprised to recognize grasshoppers, cockroaches,
beetles, flies, bees, butterflies and even moths. For an
instant, he doubted that they were really back in
Jurassic times. It seemed incredible that modern-day
insects could have had their beginnings so very long
ago. As if to add proof to his thoughts, a large ant
crawled over the side of the jeep and he watched its
frantic progress across the windshield.

Moisture clung to the giant leaves of the plants,
slapping water at them as the jeep pushed aside the
heavy foliage. Clinging close to the earth like a thick
layer of gas, a heavy whitish mist silently worked its
meandering way among the plants.

A silence seemed to pervade the air, a silence as
deep as the lush growth, a silence somehow frightening in its completeness. It was almost as if life had
withdrawn into a hollow shell, peering out with wide
eyes. There was the feeling of being watched, a
feeling as terrifying as the sound of footsteps behind
you in a dark alley. The silence was broken only by
the throaty growl of the truck and the higher-pitched
whine of the jeep. And these sounds were completely
out of place in this primitive expanse of wilderness.
The mechanical voice of a rumbling engine was almost
a violation here.

There was a magnificence to the scene, a lordly
grandeur that filled Chuck with strange, excited
emotions. Everything around him seemed to be growing without purpose or plan. The land fairly shrieked
disorder, and yet, strangely enough, there was a

deeper feeling of harmony about the whole. It puzzled Chuck and it confused him.

He kept watching the tortured progress of the truck, Pete's red head shining above the tailgate like a bobbing beacon.

Unconsciously, his eyes strayed from the truck to the perimeter of heavy growth beyond the truck. He blinked, looked again, and then opened his eyes wide.

"Owen!"

"What is it?"

"Look! Past the truck. Near those evergreens!"

"What is it, Chuck?" Owen stood up and peered over the windshield, his eyes serious.

"Stegosaurs!" Chuck said. "He's leading us right at them, Owen. A herd of stegosaurs!"

Chapter 4 Hasty Flight

T almost the same instant, Masterson stuck his head from the cab of the truck, a beaming smile covering his face. "Look at that!" he shouted. "There are some dinosaurs for you!"

The stegosaurs were still nothing more than huge, grayish blobs set against the thick green background. Chuck looked at them again, squinting his eyes for a better view. The vehicles kept moving closer to the grazing herd.

"Turn back!" Owen shouted, his voice shrill and piercing. "Those animals can be dangerous, Masterson."

Masterson began laughing—a highly, penetrating laugh that echoed over the land.

"Masterson!" Owen shouted.

Masterson did not answer. The truck kept moving forward, and Chuck found himself unable to sit still. He kept his eyes glued to the herd. He jiggled his feet against the floor board of the jeep, clenched and unclenched his fists, nibbled at his lower lip. They were much closer now, far too close for comfort.

"Masterson!" Owen shouted again.

Masterson's head appeared. "What is it, Spencer?"

"You don't know what you're doing. Those brutes . . ."

"Brutes?" Masterson scoffed. "They're eating grass, Spencer. They're just big cows, that's all."

Owen shouted, "They're plant eaters, yes—but even herbivorous animals can stampede. Masterson, can't you . . ." He stopped talking as Masterson's head disappeared within the cab. He turned to Chuck in exasperation, a tired expression pulling at the corners of his mouth.

"We can't stop him, Chuck," he said. "It's no use."

"Maybe . . . maybe it'll be all right. They *are* plant eaters."

"Sure," Owen said, "but take a look at them." He pointed over the windshield, and Chuck followed the line his arm and outstretched finger made.

The stegosaurs were huge, truly huge. They stood on the horizon like enormous gray boulders. Chuck stared at the grotesque brutes. They were something out of a madman's imagination, something to tax the most creative mind. Their heads were close to the ground, small beaklike affairs that nibbled at the plants. Two short legs supported the front end of the beast, and from there on nature seemed to go berserk. Arcing up from the head in a high, curving line, the animal's back rose like a half-submerged island. Two rows of jutting plates, hard bones that stood out on the creature's back like a low mountain range, ran from the back of the head down the length of the tail. The tail was long and powerful, and where the bone plates ended, several sets of sharp, pointed spikes rose up to take their place. Chuck estimated the length of the stegosaurs at somewhere between fifteen and eighteen feet. The animals tilted forward precariously like clowns walking on their hands. Their hind legs were easily twice as long as their forelegs, giving them a peculiar off-balance look, as if they would fall forward on their small, hard faces at any moment. They moved ponderously, working their way among the plants, nibbling, moving on to another plant, nibbling again.

Chuck knew that the brains of these animals weighed no more than two and a half ounces, judging from the scientific measurement of the cranial cavity. He knew, too, that their total weight was greater than that of any elephant, and that an elephant's brain averaged about eight pounds—sometimes going as high as eleven pounds. The weight of an elephant's brain was seventy times that of a stegosaur's. This gave the stegosaur an intelligence approximately equal to that of a three weeks' old kitten, comparing size for size.

Chuck stared at the powerful tail with its spiked end, knowing this tail could be wielded with lethal effectiveness. In an age of reptiles with gashing teeth and ripping claws, in an age where flesh-eating dinosaurs ranged the earth preying on their weaker numbers, the stegosaur's only weapon was his effective armor plate and his powerful tail. Chuck shuddered as he thought of it in action. Then he realized just how close they were to the animals.

"Owen! For Pete's sake, he's practically driving into their mouths!"

Owen was about to answer when the truck ahead squealed to a stop, the tires gripping futilely at the slippery vegetation. Masterson leaped from the cab, the gun clutched tightly in one hand. He began walking back toward the jeep, his hat tilted back on his head, his black curly hair spilling over onto his forehead.

"Hey, Spencer!" he called.

Owen climbed down out of the jeep, his eyes on the quietly grazing herd less than a hundred yards away.

"What is it?" he asked.

"These animals. What do you call them?"

"Stegosaurs," Owen answered. "They're dangerous, Masterson. They can use their tails like . . ."

"What was that name again?"

"Stegosaurs."

"Does the name mean anything?"

"Yes. It means 'roofed lizard.'"

"Say," Masterson said. "That's clever. With all those bones sticking out of his back, I can see where he got the name. Roofed lizard, huh?"

Owen tried a new tack. "Look, Mr. Masterson, let's turn around and get out of here. These babies are nothing to play with, believe me."

"I don't intend playing with them," Masterson said sharply. "Roofed lizard," he repeated, apparently fascinated by the name. An engaging grin broke over his face, spilling white teeth onto his ruddy features. "How would you like a roofed lizard for one of your museums?"

"We've got some, thanks," Owen said. "There's a

beautifully mounted skeleton in the Yale University
Museum, for that matter. And there are . . ."

"A *skeleton*," Masterson said, still smiling. "I mean
the real McCoy. A trophy. Flesh and bones, Spencer.
How does that appeal to you?"

"It doesn't. It's against the law, Masterson, and you
know it."

The smile dropped from Masterson's face, and his
lips set in a tight line. "Laws are made to be broken,"
he said.

"That's where we don't see eye to eye," Owen
answered.

"And that's what makes horse races," Masterson
countered.

Chuck watched Owen's fists clench into tight, hard
balls and he fully expected his brother to haul off at
Masterson. Instead, Owen calmly replied, "It's a little
difficult to think of man-made laws when you're so
far away from them, Masterson. I warn you, though,
that the punishment for what you plan to do is
extremely severe. If I were you, I'd turn that truck
around and head back to the rendezvous site."

"He's right, Mr. Masterson," Arthur said from
behind the wheel of the jeep.

Masterson turned slowly, his eyes cold. "I think,"
he said slowly, "that you'd best keep your opinions
to yourself, Arthur." He turned back to Owen and
said, "I'm going to shoot one of your roofed lizards,
Spencer. Right between the eyes."

"Think you'll be able to do it?" Owen asked.

Masterson began chuckling, and Chuck looked in
amazement at this man whose emotions could range
from seething hatred to jocularity in the space of ten

seconds. "This gun could fell a charging elephant, Spencer," he said, holding out his weapon.

"These aren't elephants," Owen said. "A stegosaur has more armor than a heavy tank!"

Masterson smiled charmingly. "I've stopped tanks in my time, too, Spencer. Just watch me." He turned crisply, striding away from the jeep, heading back for the truck with long steps.

"He's crazy," Chuck blurted. "He's absolutely out of his mind!"

The truck started, lurching forward over the ground to a low, flat clearing that edged on the feeding stegosaurs. One of the beasts glanced up as the truck approached, its huge spiked tail flicking heavily to one side, thumping against a thick cycad. Then it lowered its head and continued to nibble at the low shrubbery.

The truck crept to within fifty feet of the herd, while Arthur cautiously guided the jeep behind it. Still, the stegosaurs paid no attention to the intruders. Their jagged, arching backs jutted up grotesquely over the vegetation like animated stone walls, but they continued to feed calmly.

The truck stopped, and Masterson climbed out of the cab, the thick plants beginning some ten feet from where he stood on the flatland. Chuck heard an ominous click as Masterson shoved a shell into the chamber. There was another click as the safety catch yielded to Masterson's thumb. Masterson fell to one knee, his head cocked, the gun in firing position.

"He's going to shoot!" Owen whispered. Then, as if suddenly realizing what was about to happen, he started running forward. "Masterson! Hold your fire. Hold your . . ."

The shot bellowed into the afternoon silence like the roar of a wounded giant. It echoed from the trees, spread over the rocks, carried its message of lethal doom to anything that heard and anything that would listen.

Chuck felt his fingernails bite into his palms. He didn't take his gaze from the stegosaurs. He saw one of the animals lift its head and stare around stupidly. Owen was almost upon Masterson now.

"You double-plated idiot!" he shouted.

Masterson didn't look up. He triggered off another fast shot. This time he hit his target.

A terrifying bellow split the air. It tore at the nerves and splintered the silence. It was the very essence of primitiveness. It was a bellow of sheer, raw pain. It stifled the senses like the cry of a madman in a padded cell. Chuck saw one of the stegosaurs lift its head quickly, the gigantic tail lashing out like a spiked, bloated bull-whip.

"I hit him!" Masterson shouted. "I hit him!"

"Get back to the truck, you fool!" Owen said.

Gardel was leaning out of the cab, his eye pressed to the telescopic sight on his own gun. Pete had climbed into the front of the truck and was sitting behind the wheel. He winced, pulling his head between his shoulders, as Gardel's gun added its thunder to Masterson's.

The stegosaurs turned away from their food now, their small heads coming up, their bodies turning ponderously as the shots spattered around them. The ground erupted in showery cascades of mud and vegetation as the heavy slugs ripped into it. Another reptile bellowed in pain, and Gardel shouted exultantly from the cab of the truck.

And then it started.

It was almost imperceptible at first. It was as if all the reptiles had suddenly decided to shift their position at once. They turned slowly like comedians in a dead-pan routine, their powerful tails swinging around, their humped backs bobbing like ships on a sea of vegetation. They began to move forward slowly. They kept their heads low. Their ridiculously short legs stamped on the ferns. They moved like an outlandish football team struggling for a first down or a group of drunken lumberjacks staggering down out of the mountains. But they moved with purpose—a dim, primitive purpose spawned in a group of infinitesimal brains. Something was troubling them. They must defend themselves against this something.

Masterson shrieked in delight as the beasts began moving out of the shrubbery toward the clearing. Owen tugged at his arm, but Masterson shoved him aside angrily. He raised the rifle, fired rapidly, then reloaded and continued to trigger off shot after shot into the herd.

The stegosaurs moved deceptively. What appeared to be a halting, stumbling gait was suddenly a headlong flight. They moved through the ferns like a gigantic Juggernaut, their five-toed forelegs pounding against the earth, their tails thumping behind them. They formed a solid wall of destruction that charged blindly ahead, uprooting cycads, crushing rocks, setting the earth to trembling. The din was ear-shattering. It was like a thousand sledge hammers

turned loose at once or a million bowling balls upsetting ten million pins in a million hollow alleys.

The crack of Masterson's high-powered rifle
sounded small and ineffective in the thunderstorm of
the huge reptiles' hoofs.

Suddenly Masterson seemed to come awake to the
danger. He got to his feet rapidly and began running
for the truck. Gardel kept firing from the cab. Owen
sprinted for the jeep as the stegosaurs charged into
the clearing, bellowing wildly, blind rage guiding their
powerful muscles

"Get this baby started," Chuck said to Arthur. There
was an undertone of anxiety in his voice. He wet his
lips as the stegosaurs roared forward, trampling over
the spot Owen and Masterson had just left.

Chuck heard the motor whine as Arthur stepped on
the starter. Owen reached the jeep and hopped aboard.

"Let's get out of here," he panted. "Fast!"

The stegosaurs stopped, raising their heads, seeming to sniff the air for their enemy. Arthur tried the
starter again. A complaining moan came from beneath
the hood of the jeep.

"What's the matter?" Owen asked. He watched the
stegosaurs as they lowered their heads again.

"I . . . something's wrong. She . . . she . . ." Arthur
swallowed hard, glanced up briefly at the herd of
reptiles.

"What is it?" Chuck fairly shouted.

"She won't start!" Arthur blurted. "Something's
wrong with her." He looked at Chuck helplessly. When
he spoke again, his voice was edged with panic. "She
just won't start!"

Chapter 5 Escape Plans

WELL . . ." Owen wiped a hand over his face, cutting himself short. He glanced uneasily over the windshield. The truck had already begun to move out of the clearing, and the stegosaurs studied the area with dull, unintelligent eyes, seeking a new prey.

Arthur's hands were trembling, but he climbed out of the jeep in spite of his fear, walking to the front and lifting the hood quickly. He looked over his shoulder at the mountainous beasts and then ducked his head over the engine.

Chuck was beside him instantly. He'd taken apart his own hot rod so many times that he knew engines the way he knew his own name. He'd never tinkered with a jeep, though, and he'd never had a herd of dinosaurs looking over his shoulder while he worked.

"What is it?" Arthur asked. There was concern in his voice, but the panic was gone now.

"I think the plugs are wet. Driving through all that wet shrubbery probably did it. We'll need a rag."

Arthur didn't hesitate a moment. He seized his shirt at the top and ripped it over his head. He pushed it off his arms and handed it to Chuck. "Hurry," he said simply.

Chuck glanced at the stegosaurs. They were beginning to move again, slowly, just the way they had before. They moved toward the jeep, their awkward gait looking almost comical.

Chuck took the T-shirt and began drying the plugs. "Get back in the jeep," he said. "Start her up. We haven't got time to waste."

Arthur ran around the side and hopped in behind the wheel. He stepped on the starter.

Nothing.

"Keep trying!" Chuck shouted. He wiped at the spark plugs frantically, drying them carefully, soaking up the water that clung to the engine, too.

Arthur tried again. There was a faint cough, a sputter and the exasperating, wailing whine again.

The stegosaurs were gaining speed. The earth began to shake as they swung around toward the jeep, great clods of mud and greenery bursting into the air beneath their hoofs.

Chuck ran to the other side of the jeep, tossing open the hood and starting on the spark plugs there. Arthur tried the starter again. The sound was lost in the overwhelming thunder of the approaching reptiles. There was another timid cough, a sputter, and Chuck saw the fan belt whirl as the engine caught. He leaped onto the fender, the hood still open, and shouted, "Let 'er rip!"

Arthur backed the jeep in a wide, screaming curve

as the stegosaurs closed the distance. He turned the
wheel sharply and jammed his foot against the accelerator. The jeep jerked forward like a bullet from a
pistol, narrowly missing a cycad, almost knocking
Chuck loose from his precarious perch on the fender.

The stegosaurs trampled past in a cloud of mud,
ferns and flying leaves. The jeep bounced as the
armored tons of flesh shook the ground. There was a
whirl of gray and green and agitated brown. Suddenly
the stegosaurs were gone and the jeep was scrambling
across the clearing like a frightened rabbit, Chuck
clinging to the fender for dear life.

Arthur stopped the jeep for a moment while Chuck
leaped to the ground and onto the seat in one quick
motion. The jeep lurched forward again. Behind them,
the stegosaurs wheeled for another charge. The truck
had stopped at the edge of the clearing, and Chuck
could see Masterson and Gardel leaning over the tailgate, firing at the animals behind the jeep.

When the jeep got closer, the truck started moving
again, with rifle fire erupting in sharp, even cracks
from the tailgate and small blossoms of yellow sprout-
ing from the hot barrels.

Arthur kept his big, brown hands firmly on the
wheel as he followed the truck around the clearing and
through the ferns. The noise of the stegosaurs was
growing fainter, and Chuck knew they would soon
outdistance the lumbering beasts.

Arthur turned to him then and said softly, "Sometimes, life gets mighty hard to live. Sometimes. But it's
good to be alive anyway." There was gratitude in his
deep brown eyes and a serious expression on his strong
features.

Chuck didn't say anything. He was remembering how Arthur had unhesitatingly jumped out of the jeep and thrown open the hood. He was remembering, too, the way the stegosaurs had looked as they massed for a charge. A shudder worked its way through his body.

"It's all over," Owen said quietly. "For now, anyway."

Chuck looked back over his shoulder. Far in the distance, beyond the herd of stegosaurs, he saw two sharply pointed white rocks jutting up against the sky. The rocks were large, like two oversized mounds of vanilla custard plopped down on a green plate. They sat there majestically, placid against the mild blue sky. Chuck looked at them hard, remembering every detail of them. He knew that the rendezvous site was near those towering rocks and he didn't want to forget that.

The stegosaurs had stopped running and were already intent on nibbling at the foliage again. It was almost as if their small brains could cope with only one problem at a time. The only problem that confronted them at the moment was their hunger. They looked almost docile as they stood with their heads bent, plucking at the leaves.

They're real, Chuck thought. *Really real.*

Up to this point, they had been creatures of the imagination. They weren't any longer. They were as real as cats or dogs, as real as anything Chuck had ever known. The pictures in the books had come alive for him at last. The word "stegosaur" would never again be simply a word. Whenever he saw it, he would remember the herd in flight, remember the sound of their hoofs, remember with horror the first terrifying scream when one of Masterson's bullets had found a mark.

And there were others, wallowing in the inland lakes, feeding on the plants, chewing the smaller animals to shreds. Everywhere around them, a universe of reptiles, a society of lumbering beasts.

Where, he wondered.

And *when?*

Would *Allosaurus* suddenly rush from the forest, his giant jaws snapping, his claws bared?

How many reptiles watched from the depths of their primitive shelters, their flat eyes following the slow progress of the two vehicles?

The thought was a little frightening. Chuck suddenly wished he were back home, in his own time, in his own room, with only his books to remind him of Jurassic times.

One week. If everything went well, they'd be home in one week. *If* everything went well. But if Masterson insisted on his foolish plans, if he continued to shoot at every reptile he saw . . . Chuck didn't want to think about it.

The land was sparsely vegetated now, leveling off into beds of limestone and shale. Several ferns dotted the rocks, but these were few and far between. It was like leaving a thick living-room rug and walking out to the sidewalk. The going was easier, and the truck picked up speed, its tires rolling easily over the rock beds. Arthur kept the jeep about fifty feet behind the truck. He hadn't said anything for a long time. He kept his eyes on the truck's tailgate, watching Masterson and Gardel. Both men spoke animatedly, pointing to animals that appeared briefly in the distance.

The truck swung around in a wide arc, and a large lake came into view, shimmering blue in the bright light of the afternoon sun. The truck stopped, and Masterson dropped to the ground and waved at the jeep. Arthur stepped on the gas pedal, bringing the jeep up alongside the truck.

Masterson was smiling. "Quite a tussle back there, eh, Spencer?"

Owen didn't answer.

"What's the matter, Spencer? Angry about something?"

"You almost got us all killed," Chuck blurted.

"We're still alive, aren't we?"

"Through no fault of yours," Owen spoke up.

"Come on," Masterson said cheerfully. "Forget about it, will you? This can be fun for all of us."

"Sure," Owen said dully. "Loads of good, clean fun."

Masterson waved his arm at the lake. "How's this for a camp site, Spencer?"

"Are you really asking my advice or just telling me you plan to camp here?"

"Come on, Spencer," Masterson said again. "No need to be surly about this. I really want your advice."

"My advice is to turn the truck around and head back for the rendezvous site. Once we get there, my advice is to stick close to the vehicles for the next week. That's my advice."

"Your advice isn't very good," Masterson said dryly. "Forgive me for asking." He turned on his heel and shouted, "Brock, break out the supplies. We're camping here for the night!"

They watched Pete climb out of the truck and walk around to the tailgate. Together with Gardel, he began unloading tents, cooking utensils, cartons of food. Gardel moved quickly, like a dark shadow that flitted in the afternoon sun.

"I'd better go help," Arthur said. He was sliding off the seat of the jeep when Masterson turned and began walking toward them. He stopped alongside the jeep as Arthur swung out from behind the wheel.

"Arthur," he said softly.

"Yes, Mr. Masterson?"

Chuck felt every muscle in his body tense. There was a strange look on Masterson's face, a tight smile accompanied by a glitter in his brown eyes.

"How about getting over to the truck and lending a hand?" he asked.

"I was just headed . . ."

"Never mind what you were just about to do. Get over to the truck." Masterson's voice was ugly.

"Sure," Arthur said dully. He dropped to the ground and began walking toward the truck. He had draped his soiled shirt over his shoulders, and his muscles rippled in the sunlight as he walked, his shoulders broad under the thin material.

Masterson watched him go, and then turned to Owen and Chuck. There was a smile on his face.

"There was no need for that," Owen said.

"I pay a man to work," Masterson answered, "and I expect work."

"We disagree about a lot of things, Mr. Masterson," Chuck said.

Masterson shrugged. "Don't misunderstand me. Arthur's a good worker. One of the best I've ever had. But . . ."

"Sure," Owen said.

Masterson looked at Owen's face. Then his eyes flicked to Chuck's. He found no friendliness there. Chuck watched a puzzled frown cross Masterson's features and he realized again that the big man simply did not understand.

Masterson shrugged again and made a slight shaking motion with his head. "Well," he said, "I hope you two snap out of your little peeves. It'll make things a lot more pleasant."

He turned without saying another word, heading back for the truck. Pete had already started a fire, and a pot of coffee was brewing on it.

"We've got to get out of here," Owen said.

Chuck nodded, still thinking of Masterson, wondering what went on in the man's mind.

"If we can get back to the rendezvous site, we may be able to get word to the authorities."

"Shouldn't they already know what happened, Owen?"

Owen shook his head. "I don't see how. The Time Slip is fully automatic. They won't be picking us up for a week. They've no way of knowing what Masterson has done."

"But . . ." Chuck paused, suddenly aware that they were both whispering. "If we can't get back for a week, how are we going to contact the authorities?"

"I figure there are plenty of government-sponsored scientists roaming the Jurassic period," Owen explained. "Maybe some of them are due for pickup at about this time. If we can catch them at the rendezvous site, we can give them a message to take back."

Chuck shook his head dubiously. "Sounds like a long

gamble to me. After all, you don't know for sure that anyone is scheduled for pickup right now."

"I realize that. But it's a chance."

"Yeah," Chuck said listlessly. "It's a chance."

"Maybe we can get away when it's dark," Owen said. "Masterson certainly doesn't expect us to take off."

Chuck glanced up quickly. "Speak of the devil."

Masterson was walking toward the jeep. He stopped and put his hands on his hips. "Unless you two are on a diet, Pete will have some grub rustled up in a little while," he said.

"Thanks," Owen said.

"You know, Spencer, I've been thinking over what you said. Maybe you're right. It is dangerous out here."

"Then you'll turn back?" Owen asked, a spark of hopefulness in his eyes.

"Well—no. But Gardel and I have decided to take turns at guard duty tonight." He paused and smiled. "Just to make sure nothing gets into the camp, you understand."

Owen's face fell. "Sure. I understand."

"And, of course," Masterson went on, "we wouldn't want anything to leave the camp, either."

"Of course," Owen said dryly. He exchanged glances with Chuck, and there was a defeated bitterness in his eyes.

"You might come over for a snack whenever you're ready," Masterson said agreeably. "I'd like you by the fire, anyway, before it gets dark." He paused and the smile grew larger on his face. "I wouldn't want any animals to carry you off."

Chapter 6 The Mighty Beasts

HE sun, a fiery ball that knew no time, poked at the night sky with a probing, red finger. The stars fled, trailing the blackness behind them, seeking safety from the blazing invader. The moon faded like a half-forgotten portrait of a loved one, and the sun rustled its tresses, sent dazzling locks of orange, yellow, red streaking across the sky. It lifted its head, and the land came alive with its brilliance. The leaves spread wide with glistening dewdrops. The animal sounds began. The mist rose, hung over the plants like a gray shroud and crumbled beneath the penetrating glare of the orange ball that hung in the sky.

And the beasts lumbered from the caves and the lakes, stretched their muscles, blinked their eyes and went forth to greet the new day.

There was the smell of coffee brewing and the low crackle of a wood fire. The ground was damp, but the inside of the sleeping bag was warm and comfortable. The coffee smell invaded Chuck's nostrils, clung to his senses with delicious warmth. He stirred, blinked his eyes, rolled over.

The sizzle of frying bacon reached his ears, followed immediately by the tangy, succulent aroma of the meat as it turned brown in the pan. Chuck's eyes opened wide and, for a moment, he thought he was back in his own room, with Mom preparing breakfast in the kitchen, and the house warm and secure with the smells of early morning baking.

He closed his eyes and thought of home, and he allowed the dream to fill his mind and his body.

> *I've always been a cook-oh, a cook-oh, that's me!*
> *Hi-ho, diddle-ee-oh,*
> *One, two, three.*

The voice was loud, but it was also mellow. Chuck kept his eyes closed and he listened to it, pretending it was the radio resting on the kitchen cabinet. He didn't want to stir. He knew where he was now, but he didn't want to shatter the dream.

> *I've cooked for kings and sailors,*
> *Bankers,*
> *Tailors; I've even cooked for jailers,*
> *A heck of a cook is me!*
> *Hi-ho, diddle-ee-oh,*
> *One, two, three.*

He knew it was Pete singing to the early morning air as he prepared breakfast for the party. There was

an innocent exuberance in Pete's voice, a complete
detachment from all problems, large or small. Chuck
yanked down the zipper on the front of his sleeping
bag and propped himself on his elbows. He listened
to Pete and a smile broke out on his face.

I've cooked in pots and roasters,
Fryers,
Toasters; I've even cooked in coasters,
A heck of a cook is me!
Hi-ho, diddle-ee-oh,
One, two, three.

As Chuck squirmed his way out of the sleeping bag,
Pete looked up, cutting his song short.

"Don't stop on my account," Chuck said quickly.

Pete chuckled softly, his green eyes crinkling at the
edges. He ran one stubby hand through his bright red
hair and said, "I was about running out of choruses,
anyway."

Chuck walked over to the fire and held out his hands
to it. "How many choruses are there?"

"I don't suppose anyone has ever counted them,"
Pete said. "I know at least thirty myself."

"Really?"

"And I've only been cooking a short time. Why,
there are cooks who could prepare a banquet and
never run out of choruses the whole while."

Chuck shook his head in appreciation of the feat
and looked around the camp. "Are we the only
two up?"

"No," Pete said. "Mr. Masterson left with Arthur
a little while ago. Said he wanted to look over the

countryside. Brock's in the back of the truck with a rifle across his knees." Pete chuckled again and shook his head. "Don't know what he expects to shoot."

"Is my brother up?" Chuck asked.

"Oh, yes, almost forgot. Masterson woke him and asked him to go along, too."

"I see." Chuck considered this a moment. Masterson was certainly going at this hunting business with all he had. He began to wonder if the force field accident had really been an accident. For a man who'd planned to take only pictures, Masterson had certainly come prepared with a junior armory. He shrugged this aside and turned his head as he heard the shuffle of feet behind him.

Denise walked quickly to the fire, hugging herself against the morning chill.

"Good morning," Chuck said.

"Good morning," she answered. She held her hands out to the fire and said, "Are Jurassic times really colder or do they just seem that way?"

"As a matter of fact," Chuck said, "they're much warmer. The dampness will go as soon as the sun has had a chance to work a little. All these plants, you know."

Denise shuddered. "I wish the sun would stop loafing, then," she said.

"How about some bacon and eggs?" Pete asked. "And a steaming mug of coffee? That ought to take the chill off."

"My uncle doesn't like me to drink coffee," Denise said. She looked around the camp and asked, "Say, where is everybody?"

"Exploring," Chuck said.

"So early?" She shook her blonde head and opened her eyes in wonder. "You'd think my uncle would want to stay as far away from those brutes as possible. Sometimes I don't understand him at all." She paused and turned to Chuck. "Like shooting at those—stegosaurs, were they? You'd think he'd have more sense than that."

"Your uncle thinks he's on an African safari," Chuck said, smiling.

Denise smiled back, a warm smile that lit her entire face. "Yes, isn't it silly? A grown man playing Tarzan."

"You'd better not let *him* hear you say that, Miss," Pete said.

Denise shrugged. "I think I'll have a little coffee after all," she said.

Pete served up the bacon and eggs, poured the steaming coffee into big, white mugs. They ate hungrily, sipping at the coffee, not stopping to talk. Pete watched them with obvious enjoyment, a cook's pride sprawled all over his face.

"This is delicious, Pete," Denise said.

"Why, thank you, Miss." Pete beamed at her.

"Excellent," Chuck chimed in.

Pete's smile grew larger and he looked as if he were ready to burst into song again. He began cleaning his pots, the smile still on his face.

Chuck got to his feet and stretched. The meal had made him feel full and lazy. He glanced over at the truck in time to see Gardel swing a leg over the tailgate and drop down to the ground. Quickly, like a black snake slithering across the ground, he came up to the fire.

"That coffee I smell?" he asked.

Pete looked up. "Like a cup, Brock?"

"I could use one."

Pete took the big pot from the fire and poured a cup for Gardel. He handed it to him and asked, "Did you kill any dinosaurs for supper?" A merry twinkle sparkled in his eyes as he studied Gardel's face.

"Things were pretty quiet," Gardel said soberly, missing Pete's wit completely. He sipped at the coffee, his thin lips pulling at the rim of the cup.

"Where are we going from here?" Pete asked.

Gardel took the cup from his lips. "Hunting," he said simply.

"For what?"

Gardel hesitated a moment. "Animals. What else is there to hunt?"

"We'd be smarter hunting for a nice warm cave or something," Denise said. "Doesn't my uncle realize these animals are dangerous?"

Gardel pulled his black brows together. "That's what makes hunting interesting," he said. "Nobody hunts household pets, Denise."

"According to law," Chuck put in, "nobody hunts dinosaurs, either."

Gardel smiled a thin smile. "You sound like your brother, son."

"My brother knows this period well," Chuck said. "He explained why real hunting wasn't allowed and . . ."

Gardel chuckled a little. "Did he really expect us to believe that knocking off a few dinosaurs is going to affect the future history of mankind?"

"No, not if that were the extent of it. But how many of a species can you kill before you exterminate the entire species?"

"I wouldn't worry about that," Gardel said. "We don't intend to knock off more than our quota." He thought that was funny and began laughing, only to stop abruptly when he saw he was laughing alone. "You know," he explained, "like in hunting season."

"Let's hope we don't wind up being the *hunted*," Pete said. "Those animals yesterday looked mighty fierce."

"They didn't touch us, did they?" Gardel asked smugly.

Pete shrugged. "Maybe they weren't very hungry."

Gardel laughed halfheartedly, then glanced at his watch. "I wonder what's keeping Mr. Masterson."

It was almost as if he'd spoken the cue for a stage entrance. The words had barely left his mouth when a thrashing in the bushes announced the return of the explorers. Masterson was the first to step onto the flat shale, stamping the mud from his shining boots.

"Well," he boomed, "I see everyone's up and around. Have a good night, Denise?"

"All right, I suppose," Denise said.

"We've got a big day ahead," Masterson said cheerfully. He was smiling broadly, as if his little sortie had been a big success. Chuck's eyes sought his brother's face, found it expressionless. "Mighty interesting country hereabout," Masterson went on. "Eh, Spencer?"

"Fine country," Owen replied.

Arthur stood silently by Owen, his arms hanging at his sides, his big hands open.

"I want to get under way as soon as possible," Masterson said. He looked at Gardel. "From what I could gather, Brock, we should head out past the lake, swinging away from it about a mile from here. That sound all right to you?"

"Whatever you say, Mr. Masterson."

"Fine! Let's load up then. Pete, Arthur, get started on this mess, will you?" He rubbed his hands together. "We've got a big day ahead. A mighty big day."

The sun climbed into the sky, peering down on the moving truck and jeep like a hot, unwinking eye. It was a warm day, like a spring day back home, with the smell of rich earth and growing things in the air. The vehicles left the flat rocks and began shoving through the tangled vegetation again. Insects sprang up around them like fine clouds of dust. The ferns parted, leafy lacelike curtains that would be pressed with the weight of time to form the coal beds of the future. The progress was slow, and the land begrudged the party every inch it gave up.

Chuck sat in the jeep and watched the land unfold before them. The panorama of green stretched for miles, a gently undulating sea of growth that shifted and rolled with the mild breeze. There was a stillness on the land that somehow made it more alien. Far in the distance, Chuck could see the jagged, weathered peaks of a mountain range. And dotting the land, like glistening mirrors embedded in a green velvet carpet, were countless lakes. There were scurrying creatures in the brush—small reptiles that gleamed brightly as they scampered by. Chuck was thankful that they'd seen none of the larger animals since their brush with the stegosaurs.

And then the pterosaur appeared, quite suddenly.

At first it was nothing more than a shadow that skimmed the ground, covering the truck and moving back over the jeep.

Chuck looked up rapidly and there it was, silhouetted against the sky, the sun filtering through its membranous wings.

It was gone almost as quickly as it had appeared.

The truck stopped and Masterson came runing back to the jeep, his rifle in his hands.

"What was that, Spencer? Did you see it? A bird or something!" His face was flushed with excitement and his eyes kept flicking to the sky.

"That was a pterosaur," Owen said. "A flying reptile."

"Brother, it was something!" Masterson said.

"Probably *Rhamphorhynchus*," Chuck said. "It looked like one."

Masterson's eyes lit up, and he pointed rapidly. "It's coming back. I'm going to get a shot at that baby!"

"I wouldn't advise it," Owen said tightly.

"I've had enough of your advice," Masterson replied.

The pterosaur was winging its way back to the jeep, gliding lower and lower. It looked something like an enormous bat with a peculiarly shaped head. It had a short, stout body, a fairly long neck and a short tail. Its wings were fully spread, some four feet from wing tip to wing tip. As it fell toward the jeep, Masterson readied his rifle for a shot.

Chuck could see every detail of the creature now.

Its front limbs ended in sharp claws. One finger of each limb was enormously elongated to support the membrane, which spread like a thin web and connected with the rear limbs.

The creature's head was a long, flat, bony affair, terminating in a pointed beak at one end. The whole head gave the illusion of having been passed through a wringer. When the pterosaur opened its jaws, Chuck saw the sparkle of sharp teeth. Then the jaws snapped shut, and the reptile's shadow fell over the jeep as the creature passed directly overhead.

There was the loud *boom* of Masterson's gun breaking the stillness of the morning. The reptile's jaws opened again, and a hoarse, high scream tore the air to shreds, ran up the spine like the blood cry of a banshee. The wings flapped frantically as Masterson squeezed off shot after shot. Chuck stood by helplessly, his fists clenched tightly. Then the pterosaur gained altitude, its long shadow gliding over the land. Higher it went, and higher, flying away from the thing with the fast-flying, steel-jacketed teeth.

"Brother!" Masterson said. "That's the strangest darned bird I've ever seen!"

"It's one of the strangest flying creatures that ever existed," Chuck said. "But it's not a bird."

"Well, it certainly looked like a bird," Masterson insisted.

"We may see some birds before we leave the Jurassic period," Owen said. "As a matter of fact, the *first* feathered creatures make their appearance in these times. I don't think you'll recognize them as birds, though."

"Well," Masterson said, still dubious, "whatever that

was, I'd have liked to take it back as a trophy." He turned and started walking back toward the truck. "Hey, Brock!" he called. "Did you see that?"

The rain came at noon.

The clouds had been piling up on the horizon since about ten o'clock, darkening the sky, casting a deep pall over the land. Lightning streaks suddenly slashed through the gray overhang, illuminating the cycads and ferns with electric fury. The thunder rolled out of the mountains, shook its noisy fist at the land, and then the rain came.

It spilled out of the sky in a wet sheet that ran across the vegetation in lashing torrents. The leaves flapped in protest, raising their frantic plea to the shrieking wind and the flailing water. Roots tore at the earth, wrenched free. Evergreens turned over, rolled beneath the force of the gale. The waters began running down out of the mountains, filling the lakes, flooding the land and turning the ground into a mucky, rain-drenched quagmire. The entire party sat in the truck, listening to the wind rip at the canvas top and watching the rain sweep by outside.

And then, almost as suddenly as it had started, the rainstorm ended. The clouds pulled their tattered gray robes across the sky, trailing smokelike wisps away from the sudden rays of the sun. The earth smelled clean and fresh. The plants glistened with a million, sparkling, watery jewels.

The mighty beasts lifted their heads to sniff the air, raised their dull, flat eyes to the sun and came forth to soak up the warmth.

The storm had ended.

❋ ❋ ❋ ❋ ❋

Masterson surveyed the mud with a disgruntled eye. "Quite a mess," he said. "Quite an unholy mess."

"We'll feel better when we've had something to eat, Mr. Masterson," Pete said. He had set up a stone fireplace and started a fire with the newspapers from the truck. When the blaze was strong, he fed it from a bag of charcoal.

Owen had walked several yards from the group surrounding the fire. He returned with a worried expression on his face.

"I think we'd better find another spot for lunch," he said.

Gardel, squatting by the fire, looked up suddenly. "Why?"

"We're near a small lake, and there are sauropods in it. I don't like it."

"What the deuce are sauropods?" Gardel asked. "Some kind of fish?"

"Fish?" Owen was plainly surprised. "Maybe I'd better explain the life setup here a little more fully."

Masterson nodded. "Maybe you'd better."

"To begin with, the word 'dinosaur' covers a large group of reptiles—most of them of gigantic size. Within that group, there are further groupings, groupings that distinguish the different types of dinosaurs. For example, a stegosaur is any armored dinosaur. Sauropods are the largest of all Mesozoic reptiles. Theropods are carnivorous dinosaurs. Ceratopsians are the horned dinosaurs—none of which exist until later in geologic time."

"I don't get it," Gardel said.

"It's easy," Owen replied. "These are simply

methods of classification. For example, let's take a
horse. We can start by saying that he is a mammal. We
can then classify him as that mammal which is a horse.
And from there, we can go on to say he is a Shetland
or an Arabian or what have you. Do you follow?"

"I think I understand," Masterson said.

"In the same manner, we can pinpoint any particular
dinosaur. The stegosaurs we ran into happened to be
the genus called *Stegosaurus,* which is the type that
gave the name to the entire stegosaur group. But there
are other stegosaurs we haven't as yet seen—and may
not see."

"That sounds simple enough," Gardel said, nodding.

"Now, a pterosaur is a flying reptile. There are two
subdivisions of pterosaurs. The one we saw earlier
today was called *Rhamphorhynchus.*"

Pete's eyes opened wide. "Wow!" he said.

"About the sauropods over there," Owen said, pointing, "I think they're of the *Brontosaurus* group, though
I can't be sure at this distance. Whatever they are,
they're darned big, much bigger than the stegosaurs
we ran into yesterday, and I think we'd better get out
of here while the getting's good."

"How far away are they?" Masterson asked.

"At the edge of the lake. About a hundred yards
or so."

"They won't bother us," Masterson said calmly.

"I might be inclined to agree with you," Owen said,
"if I didn't know how trigger-happy you were. The
sauropods are plant eaters, and I doubt if they'd be
very interested in us as food."

"I'm not interested in them, either," Masterson
assured Owen. "Don't worry about them."

"Did somebody mention food?" Denise asked, trying to lift the conversation out of the menacing route it was taking.

"Be ready in a few minutes," Pete said. He stood over the fire, stirring a huge caldron of hot soup. He was reaching over for a ladle when the shadow fell over the ground again.

Masterson leaped to his feet instantly, his eyes turning eagerly to the sky. "Another one!" he shouted. "Another of those pterosaurs." His face flushed with excitement as he sprinted for the truck. "Where's my rifle?"

"You just said you weren't going to do any more shooting," Owen said desperately.

"I didn't say anything like it," Masterson yelled over his shoulder. He had his rifle and was already ramming cartridges into the loading chamber.

"The sauropods . . ." Chuck started, but Masterson had lifted the rifle to his shoulder and was taking aim at the pterosaur overhead. When the rifle shot came, it was loud and echoing. It seemed to fill the land with its angry bellow.

"I'll get it this time," Masterson muttered. He swung around as the reptile drifted past, sighting along the barrel of his gun.

"Masterson," Owen said. "The sauropods! Your fire is attracting . . ."

"Shut up, Spencer!" Masterson snapped. He squeezed the trigger, and another shot burst on the air, reverberating in every hollow of the land. The echoes were a long time dying, but before they were gone, another sound had replaced them.

The sound was low and steady like the sodden beat of a tom-tom. It got louder as they listened, seemed to expand until it rolled like thunder.

Owen took one look in the direction of the lake. Then he turned his head and his voice was deadly cold when he spoke.

"They're coming, Masterson," he said. "And your popgun isn't going to be much help this time."

Chapter 7 Trapped

HUCK's eyes followed his brother's. He looked at the sauropods as they tramped out of the lake. Owen had been right in his first guess; they were brontosaurs, some of the largest of the reptiles. He listened to the sound of their ponderous hoofs as they pounded against the earth, and he thought they had been named correctly: brontosaurs, thunder lizards.

Thunder lizards they were. Mighty thunder lizards that rumbled forward with an awkward gait. Thunder lizards with all the fury of a storm behind them. Thunder lizards that could crush the jeep, smash the truck, tear the expedition asunder.

These were no stegosaurs. Compared to these beasts, the stegosaurs with their armored backs and tails seemed like barnyard pets. No, these were real dinosaurs, the dinosaurs everyone automatically pictured whenever the word was mentioned. They barged up out of the lake, dripping vegetation from their jaws.

The land trembled, and the party was gripped in the clutches of a tight, unreasoning fear.

They looked like islands on legs. From the tips of their small heads to the ends of their long, bulky tails, they measured more than sixty-five feet. Their backs were humped in the center, giving the illusion of a mountain with a weathered, rounded peak. Their color was a dull green, the color of bread mold or tarnished metal. They moved rapidly for their size. Their weight: thirty-eight tons! Thirty-eight *tons* of powerful muscle and ponderous bone. Thirty-eight tons of fury and stupidity that now sought the source of the explosions.

Their necks were ludicrously long, a good twenty feet from the creature's snout to the curved beginning of the mountainous back. The tail was equally long, and if there had been a head on the end of it, it would have been difficult to tell one end of the animal from the other.

Chuck knew which end was which at the moment.

The end that was bearing down on them with remarkable rapidity was the front. The other end carried a powerful tail that could probably knock the underpinnings from the Empire State Building!

Figures were figures and they meant nothing. They were only numbers until they were compared to other known figures. The creatures were more than sixty-five feet long. What was sixty-five feet? A number, yes. But more. It was a locomotive engine attached to a railroad car. It was a good-sized swimming pool. It was a three-story house laid on its side.

Chuck didn't have to compare thirty-eight tons with anything. He knew what thirty-eight tons added up to. Two thousand pounds in a ton, and he weighed 160 pounds. He weighed 160 pounds and each of the creatures charging for the camp weighed at least 76,000 pounds! That was a lot of beef—an awful lot of beef—and it was all angry; it was all destructive and it was all intent on doing something about these people who made disturbing noises with rifles.

The fear gave way to the need for immediate action. They began to run. They would have run straight into the thundering herd if Owen hadn't shouted, "This way! To the rocks!"

The rocks rose like a beckoning fortress a few hundred feet from the camp. They weren't high, but they were long, set like the thousands of stone walls that dot New England. Ferns and mosses grew around and over the natural barrier, and it was a little hard to see exactly where the rocks ended. But they offered protection—a wall behind which to hide from the murderous, trampling limbs of the brontosaurs.

They began running, Owen leading the way, Pete behind him, Denise next, then Arthur and Chuck. Only Masterson turned in the opposite direction. There was fear in his eyes, an unmasked fear that told Chuck the erstwhile hunter hadn't expected anything quite like this. Firing at a stegosaur was one thing and firing at a fragile-looking pterosaur was another. But a brontosaur was a mountain on legs. No man in his right mind stood and fired at a moving mountain.

The party straggled across the countryside like the tail of a kite, running, stumbling, reaching for the rocks. Behind him, Chuck heard the whine of the jeep's engine as Masterson started it. He turned his head, still running, in time to see the jeep back away from the truck and head off in the other direction, away from the rocks.

The word "coward" crossed his mind rapidly, but he shoved it aside when he caught sight of the brontosaurs again. They weren't bothering with the jeep They had swerved and were heading for the majority of the party now. They were headed for the group that staggered toward the rock barrier.

"Owen!" Chuck shouted.

Owen stopped dead in his tracks. Pete stumbled past him, intent on reaching the rocks, and Arthur took Denise's hand and dragged her after him. It didn't take Owen long to see what was going to happen. Even the rocks would offer poor protection if the herd decided to trample them into the ground.

Chuck had started to run back for the truck and he glanced back over his shoulder to see that Owen was following him. He had reached the truck and started the engine when Owen popped into the cab beside him. They didn't waste many words.

"What's your plan?" Owen asked.

"Cut them off. Drive around them and try to head them the other way." Chuck spoke rapidly, his voice hoarse.

He had already started the truck in motion, turning the wheels toward the charging brontosaurs.

"Right," Owen said. He swung out onto the running board and climbed the slats into the back of the truck. When he returned, he was carrying a rifle.

The truck rolled forward, bouncing over the pockmarked ground, driving in a straight line between the enraged herd and the rock barrier. Chuck couldn't see any of the party, and he assumed they were down low behind the wall, flat against the trembling ground.

The huge dinosaurs kept coming. They had a new quarry now; a dull brown truck that moved across the ground and somehow resembled one of the smaller lizards. The brontosaurs knew how to dispose of other annoying reptiles. It was simple. Step on them. Step on them until they were broken and crushed and unable to move. This was the law of the times, survival of the fittest, the weak against the strong. They had felt the terrible teeth of the carnivores, had learned to seek refuge in the deeper water when *Allosaurus* showed on the horizon, his claws bared, his jaws snapping. But when they fought, they fought with their bodies, using their enormous bulk to stamp out resistance. This thing that rolled across the ground was the thing that had spoken with a booming voice. It should be crushed and therefore eliminated. It was as simple as that.

From behind the wheel of the truck, it didn't look quite as simple. Chuck saw only the massive wall of green flesh as it rumbled forward, long necks bobbing, tails thumping. He thought of how easily that wall could crush the truck, and the thought sent an ache to his throat. He swung the truck in a wide circle and then headed back for the herd.

"Here goes nothing!" he shouted.

Owen was smiling as he leaned out of the cab, the rifle ready for firing. "It's been nice knowing you, world," he said.

Chuck kept his foot pressed tight on the accelerator. Like long-lost relatives rushing to greet each other, the truck and the herd hurried across the ground. Owen's

rifle spoke once, twice. There was a short pause and
then the rifle bellowed into voice again. Chuck turned
the wheel sharply, driving for the edges of the herd,
picking one brontosaur and aiming the front of the
truck right at its middle. Owen was out of the cab now,
one foot braced on the fender, his arm looped through
the open window of the door. He kept firing, the
ejected shells streaming over his shoulder like a brass
pennant.

"They're turning!" Chuck shouted.

"Force them over," Owen replied. "Crowd them."

Chuck turned the wheel again, and the herd began
to swerve toward the right, fleeing from the pugnacious brown thing that kept barking at them. They
stumbled over each other, their huge hulks crowded
together as they made a complete turn and started
running away from the wall of rocks.

Owen kept the rifle going. He didn't bother aiming
now. Chuck knew he didn't really hope to do any
damage with the gun. Instead, he was using sound as
a weapon—and an effective one, it seemed to Chuck.
The brontosaurs were now in a frenzied flight. They
seemed to have forgotten just why they left the sanc-
tity of the lake. Their only concern was to escape the
sounds that came from everywhere around them, sharp
staccato bursts that whistled past their bobbing heads.

Chuck's hands were sweating on the wheel and he
could feel perspiration soaking his shirt, trickling down
his face. His heart was thumping against his ribs,
threatening to drown out the thunder of the dinosaurs
as they fled before the truck. His foot was clamped on
the accelerator, almost as if it were an extension of the
truck. He wasn't aware that he had clenched his lower

lip between his teeth until he tasted the salty flow of blood in his mouth.

"That's it," Owen shouted above the din. "We've got them running now, boy."

"I think we can turn back . . ." Chuck started.

The scream knifed the sky, terror and helplessness sending it into the upper register.

"What the . . ."

Chuck stared through the windshield, his eyes scanning the ground ahead. The dust rose in billowing clouds as the brontosaurs trod the earth in headlong flight.

The scream came again, a piercing, peace-shattering scream that sliced its way up Chuck's spine.

"Owen, what . . ."

Owen's eyes opened wide. "Good gravy! Masterson!"

Chuck saw it then. Masterson was sitting at the wheel of the jeep, anxiously looking over his shoulder at the advancing herd. His eyes were wide. Stark terror was etched on his face. The jeep, sunk to the hub caps in mud, was directly in the new path of the herd.

The dinosaurs were still a good two hundred yards away, but at the speed they were traveling, Masterson was as good as dead unless something was done quickly.

Chuck didn't stop to think. By all rights, Masterson was to blame for everything that had happened. If he hadn't shot at the pterosaur, he wouldn't have attracted the brontosaurs. They would not have had an angry herd of moving mountains to contend with, and he wouldn't be sitting in a useless jeep now watch-

ing death bear down on him with amazing rapidity. It
would be a sort of ironic justice if Masterson . . .

No!

Chuck turned the wheel of the truck, leaving the
herd and cutting across the terrain in a sharp diagonal
line that sliced the path of the dinosaurs' advance.
Retribution might have been good in Masterson's case,
Chuck reasoned. But there was something that flickered beneath the dictates of reason—something basic.
Masterson was a man. No matter what he'd done, he
was a man—and he was at the mercy of beasts, waiting
for his death. Something seemed to call out across the
lush stretch of ground, something as primitive as the
beasts themselves. And without hesitation, Chuck answered the call. Here in the beginnings of time, millions upon millions of years before Man evolved on
earth, Chuck sensed the bond that would eventually
set Man high above the beasts. He knew what he must
do and he did it without further thought, driving the
truck at breakneck speed to reach Masterson before
the dinosaurs did.

When he reached the jeep, he stopped just short of
the deep mud. Masterson was staring at the animals,
his face a chalky white. They were no more than a
hundred yards away now, their speed never lessening,
their hoofs setting up an unholy din.

"Come on, Masterson," Chuck shouted. "Hop in."

Masterson didn't move. He kept sitting in the jeep,
his hands frozen to the wheel, his head turned over his
shoulder to watch the approaching brontosaurs.

"Masterson!" Owen shouted. "For crying out loud,
hurry up."

Masterson swallowed, but otherwise he didn't move.

"Masterson!" This time Chuck's voice was edged with panic. The dinosaurs were getting closer every second. Unless they . . .

"I'll get him," Owen said suddenly. He put the rifle down and leaped from the truck, sinking to his knees in mud as he approached the jeep. Masterson sat in a frightened stupor, sweat standing out on his forehead, his knuckles white against the steering wheel.

"Snap out of it!" Owen shouted.

The sound of the brontosaurs was loud now. It filled the air and left room for nothing else. There was only the thunderous noise, echoing and re-echoing, hammering on the eardrums.

Owen lashed out with the open palm of his hand. The sound of the slap was lost beneath the greater roar of the animals, but Chuck saw Masterson's head snap back with the blow.

"Come on!" Owen shouted. "Come on. Masterson, for the love of . . ."

Chuck was frightened now. Fear leaped inside him like a cold, slimy thing. It clutched at his heart, set the muscles of his back twitching, tore at his mind with unnerving fingers.

"Owen—Owen—"

He didn't know what he wanted to say. His cry came out of his mouth like a hoarse plea, drowned in the noise around them.

"Owen—"

He saw his brother reach for Masterson's hands. Slowly, methodically, Owen began prying Masterson's fingers loose from the wheel. Chuck watched, counting the fingers, listening to the thunder swell, feeling the truck vibrate beneath him as the animals came closer, closer.

Two . . . three . . . five. One hand was loose.

"Come on, Masterson," Owen bellowed. He was breathing hard, the sweat staining the back of his shirt in two great, round semicircles. "Come on, you dirty . . ."

The engine of the truck stalled.

Panic gripped Chuck as he stepped on the starter. It was all a bad dream now, the worst dream he'd ever had. Everything seemed to blend together into a horrible nightmare of sound and vague impressions. It was like a madman leading a symphony orchestra in his own composition.

Beneath everything was the steady, incessant rumble of the approaching reptiles. In counterpoint to that was the whine of the starter as Chuck pressed on it. And over that was a dim view of Owen prying the remaining fingers loose, one at a time.

Six . . . seven . . . eight . . .

Chuck kept his foot pressed on the starter. He could barely hear the whine. He didn't know the motor had caught until he heard the sullen protest of the starter's teeth. He shifted his foot to the accelerator, idly wondering what had caused the truck to stall.

"I've got him!" Owen shouted.

Chuck glanced over his shoulder at the herd and then his eyes flicked to his brother. Owen was bodily dragging Masterson from the jeep. Masterson was limp, a quivering, frightened hulk of a man. His eyes were blank with fear, and his mouth had come unhinged.

Owen tossed him into the cab of the truck and stooped to pick up his rifle.

"Get going!" he shouted.

"Get in," Chuck replied anxiously. There wasn't much time. He could almost hear the breathing of the animals. He heard the rifle go off as Owen triggered a shot at the herd.

"Go on," Owen shouted, "I'll hop aboard. Move! Move!"

Chuck started the truck in motion, turning the wheel slowly, treading lightly on the accelerator. He wanted to make sure Owen could hop aboard, and he didn't want to give him a fast-moving vehicle to reach for. Behind him, he heard the rifle belch again and again. He kept the truck moving in a slow arc, curving away from the path of the herd.

Sudden realization snapped at his senses like a bull-whip!

Owen had no intention of hopping aboard. He was firing to attract the attention of the brontosaurs, firing so that the truck could make a safe escape.

Chuck acted instantly. He slammed on the brake and Masterson lurched forward drunkenly on the seat, almost smashing his head against the windshield. Chuck threw the gears into reverse, rammed his foot against the gas pedal and started to back up. His head was outside the window. What he saw made him want to die.

The beasts thundered ahead, and Owen stood directly in their path, infinitesimal compared with the monsters that bore down on him. The rifle cracked ineffectually. And then the beasts overran him, crushing him into the earth. His blond head showed for an instant beneath the rolling, trampling dull green hoofs, and then it was gone.

The sight wrenched at Chuck's eyes and he felt tears spring up instantly. His face crumbled, and there was an ache in the pit of his stomach and a heaviness around his heart. He saw the animals whirl and start forward again. Instinct told him he should start the truck and leave this danger area. He glanced once at the man sitting next to him, a seething hatred boiling up inside him like a dark, evil brew. His hand reached the gear shift, went through the motions. He turned the truck and drove, leaving the spent brontosaurs behind. He found it difficult to see because of the tears that welled up in his eyes and spilled down his cheeks.

Owen, his heart cried. *Owen, Owen, Owen.*

The party was silent when Chuck pulled the truck up beside the rock barrier. He sat behind the wheel, his eyes dry, emotion drained out of him. There was only an emptiness within him—a lonely bitterness that filled him with a dull, aching pain.

Arthur was the first to come to him.

"We saw," he said. His voice was strangely gentle. "We saw everything."

Chuck nodded silently. Gardel had come around to the other side of the truck and was shaking Masterson now. "Are you all right, Mr. Masterson? Mr. Masterson, are you all right?"

Masterson shook his head and sighed deeply, seeming to come out of his stupor all at once. "Those . . . those . . ." he stammered.

"We saw it from here," Gardel soothed him. "It must have been terrible."

"Charging down," Masterson said. "All of them. Like . . . like the end of the world."

"You shouldn't have fired at the pterosaur," Pete said suddenly. His voice was as hard as a chip of granite.

"Wh—what?" Masterson blinked at his cook.

"You caused the stampede. You killed young Owen!"

"Owen?" Masterson asked. "Me? I didn't . . ."

"What kind of fool talk is that?" Gardel wanted to know.

"As sure as if you'd used a knife on him, you killed him," Pete went on. He stood near the truck, his green eyes blazing with anger.

"I did nothing of the sort!" Masterson said firmly. "I had no idea the animals would stampede."

"Owen warned you," Arthur put in.

"I certainly didn't ask Spencer to try any fool heroics on my be—"

"How can you talk like that?" Denise suddenly shouted. "How can you be so pompously self-righteous? Don't you see what you've done? Don't you see . . ."

"I'll thank you to respect your elders," Masterson said. A deep scowl had begun on his face, and a pout was beginning to form on his thick lips.

"You're a murderer," Arthur said clearly.

"I don't have to take that talk from a lousy . . ."

"That's enough of that," Pete cut in sharply.

Masterson seemed puzzled. He turned to Chuck

and his voice got softer. "Chuck," he said, "you don't believe that, do you? You don't believe I murdered your brother."

It took Chuck a long time to answer. He was remembering Owen. He was remembering the older brother he'd loved and honored. He was remembering the times they'd had together, the fights against the neighborhood bullies, the excited sharing of new toys or games, the hushed talks they had in their room at night when the rest of the house slumbered. He was remembering this. He was also remembering the way Owen had looked just before the dinosaurs had crushed the life out of him.

His voice came at last. It was low, barely more than a whisper. "I don't think I want to talk to you, Mr. Masterson."

"Aw now, Chuck, let's be sensible about this. After all . . ."

"I said," Chuck warned, his voice rising, "that I didn't want to talk to you. Not now, not ever."

"Look . . ."

"Shut up!" Chuck shouted hysterically. "Shut up! Leave me alone, can't you?"

He felt Arthur's arm around his shoulder, and he saw Masterson shrug and climb out of the truck. He heard Gardel whisper, "Don't let this upset you, Dirk. It wasn't your fault." He closed his eyes tightly and refused to let the tears come.

After a little while he climbed out of the cab and walked to the back of the truck. He didn't look at Masterson. He took a shovel and rested it on his shoulder.

Then he went out alone to bury his brother.

Chapter 8 Forced March

IT wasn't until later that day that Chuck learned what had caused the truck to stall. He realized then why Masterson hadn't been able to get the jeep out of the mud, either. Both vehicles were out of gas. Originally intended for short excursions within the one-mile area surrounded by the force field, the vehicles had come a long way and now were bone-dry.

They made the discovery when they were ready to start back for the rendezvous site.

"You'll want us to go back at once," Arthur said. He glanced meaningfully at Masterson. "I don't think there are any objections now."

Chuck merely nodded. He still found allusions to his brother extremely painful. It was only with the greatest effort that he could keep the tears from his eyes. But it was impossible to keep the ache from his heart.

He and Arthur went to the jeep and tried to start

it. Chuck lifted the hood and checked the engine, while Arthur went to the tank, coming back with a stick that was dry.

"Here's the answer," he said. "No gas."

They walked back to the truck and checked the fuel in it. The results were the same.

"We'll walk," Chuck said simply.

"What?" Gardel protested. "All the way back to . . ."

"Chuck said we'll walk," Pete put in. He was holding a large skillet in his hands. The freckles on his face stood out in angry red blotches.

"This is crazy," Gardel said. "Just because . . ."

He saw the look in Chuck's eyes—a cold, menacing look. He shrugged and sighed deeply.

"We'll need supplies," Chuck said. He started for the rear of the truck and was suddenly aware of something that had eluded his grasp up to now. *He* was leading the group!

At first the thought was overwhelming. He almost turned and said, "Look, fellows, this is all a mistake. I can't . . ."

Then he thought of Owen and he knew why they had turned to him for leadership. It was an automatic thing, he supposed. Owen had been their leader and now Owen was gone. It was natural to turn to Owen's brother. The thought frightened him because he had never been in such a situation before. It frightened him even more because he had no idea where the rendezvous site was. He took a deep breath and climbed into the back of the truck, fervently wishing Owen were there to tell him what to do.

"Arthur," he called. "Pete! Want to take some of

this stuff? We'll each have to carry packs. I'll hand the equipment and food down and you can get it ready."

He got to work, trying not to think of Owen or of what lay ahead. Methodically, he passed most of what they'd need down to Arthur and Pete. He kept moving toward the front of the truck as he worked his way through the piles of canned food. Outside, Arthur and Pete arranged the food in heavy packs, fully realizing this would have to last them for a long while. Chuck began moving material, trying to get at the food stacked near the cab of the truck. It wasn't until he'd moved several shovels, pans and a large battery-driven power drill that he realized he was handling mining equipment. A puzzled frown crossed his face. What on earth was mining equipment doing in the truck? He dug a little deeper, shoving aside a half-dozen picks. And then he came across the box of dynamite. Surprise gave way to shock. He scratched his head worriedly. Why? Why had . . .

"Hey, Chuck," Arthur called. "Any more stuff coming?"

Chuck came to his senses. "Just a moment," he said. He stopped thinking about the dynamite and attacked the stack of food, carrying the cartons to Arthur's waiting hands. In a little while the truck was almost empty. They were leaving a lot of material behind, but they were taking all they could carry and they could do no better than that.

Chuck jumped down to the ground and swung a heavy pack onto his shoulders, tightening the straps across his chest. He saw Masterson lift a pack and slip his arms through the canvas loops. Gardel helped

him with it and then picked up his own pack. There
was one thing Chuck had forgotten. He climbed to
the back of the truck to correct his memory.

"Arthur."

"Yes?"

"Here," he said.

He held out his hand, and Arthur looked up at the
rifle Chuck was holding. "What's that for?"

"The animals around here are treacherous," Chuck
said. He glanced significantly at Masterson and then
handed Arthur another rifle. "You'd better give one
to Pete, too."

Arthur nodded, taking the rifles.

"How about us?" Gardel asked.

Chuck's eyes remained cold and impersonal. "I
think maybe you've both done enough hunting for
awhile."

"See here, youngster . . ." Masterson protested.

Arthur grinned good-naturedly, his teeth flashing
white against his brown skin. "Your license has been
temporarily revoked," he said softly. At the same time
he pulled back the bolt on his rifle, and the click of
the cartridge sounded a dull warning.

Masterson eyed the gun with contempt. "You're
still working for me," he said, his voice ominously
low.

"I quit, Mr. Masterson," Arthur said. "I quit a long
time ago."

"Why, you ungrateful . . ."

"I don't work for you any more," Arthur said, his
eyes level.

Chuck strapped a Colt .45 to his waist and took a
rifle from the truck. "I think we'd better get moving,"

he said, dropping to the ground between Arthur and
Masterson. "We'll need plenty of time to get back to
the rendezvous site."

He saw Pete sling his rifle, watched the sullen looks
on the faces of Masterson and Gardel. Denise came
up alongside him and said, "My uncle isn't very
happy, Chuck."

He didn't answer. He started walking ahead of the
group, heading in the direction he hoped was right.

Denise caught up and put her hand on his arm.
"Are you mad at me, *too*, Chuck? Just because he's
my uncle?"

Chuck shook his head. "I'm sorry, Denise," he said.
"No, I'm not mad at you. It's just . . . well . . . I
don't much care whether your uncle is happy or not.
I just don't care."

"May I walk with you then?"

"Sure." He glanced at her briefly. "Sure, Denise."

The going wasn't easy. They were on foot now and
they struggled for every inch of progress. The land
was wild and stubborn. It tore at their clothing and
their skin, rose in their path suddenly, erecting rock
barriers, tossing tangled patches of thick vegetation
at them. Pete walked ahead, swinging a meat cleaver
at the thick leaves and vines that threatened to
strangle all progress. The insects enjoyed a field day.
They bit angrily, descending in hordes, enjoying the
exposed skin. And the sun bore down relentlessly,
bathing them in its powerful rays.

The pack seemed to grow heavier. When Chuck
had strapped it on at the truck, it had felt almost
light. Its weight seemed to increase subtly as they
covered more miles. It bit into his armpits, the straps

threatening to cut off circulation. It hung on his
back like a heavy sack of stones, pulling at his back
and shoulder muscles, making his legs feel leaden
and dull.

And there was always the danger of the animals.
Chuck steered clear of any Jurassic fauna, remembering what had happened already, and anxious to avoid
any repetition. The land seemed to be alive with
reptiles of all types. Chuck recognized most of them,
but he never stopped the party for a closer look. He
knew that many of them were harmless plant eaters,
but he also recognized some of the smaller carnivorous dinosaurs. *Ornitholestes* was among these. He
glimpsed two of these six-foot-long flesh eaters striding across a flat rock surface on their hind legs, their
shorter forelegs dangling from their chests. They had
long, almost doglike snouts, and tails that accounted
for more than half their length. But he knew they
also had sharp teeth and he was not anxious to encounter them. He swung the party around, cutting
through a grove of cycads, avoiding the pair of
marauders.

The larger dinosaurs were in abundance, too. One
of the sauropods he recognized immediately was
Diplodocus. He saw the lone creature far in the distance, trodding the earth with slow, ponderous steps.
The animal measured eighty-seven feet from the tip
of its tail to the end of its snout, but it was not as
weighty as a brontosaur, despite the latter's shorter
length. *Diplodocus's* weight was clustered about its
middle, with most of its length absorbed in its extremely slender tail and neck. Its body was short and
compact, strongly resembling an elephant's, right

down to the dull gray coloring. Since the vertebrae in
the last ten feet of the animal's tail did not decrease in
size, this portion strongly reminded Chuck of a whip-
lash. He could imagine a flick of that tail in action,
and so he once again swerved the party from its course,
anxious to steer away from any encounters whatever.

Arthur apparently noticed Chuck's subtle manipula-
tion of the party. He pulled up alongside him and
said, "I don't blame you."

Chuck turned his head, lost in thought. "Huh?
What, Arthur? I'm sorry, I didn't hear you."

"I've been watching the way you're leading us
around the animals, I think it's a good idea."

Chuck nooded absently. "Some of them are very
dangerous. We've passed flesh eaters who could tear
us to shreds."

Arthur grinned and said, "No one would eat me.
My hide's too old and tough."

Chuck grinned with him, feeling his first moment
of companionship since Owen had met his death. "No
hide is too tough for a dinosaur," Chuck said. "Not
even Masterson's."

Arthur laughed out loud, a booming, contagious
laugh that rang over the land. "Funny thing about
Masterson," he said. "Since I quit, I feel more free
than I've ever felt. You know what I mean?"

"Well, no. Not exactly."

"There are only so many jobs a—a fellow like me
can get," Arthur said, his eyes serious, his face
thoughtful. "I'm not blaming anyone, you understand. I know that conditions sometimes get out of
hand and then the job of putting them back in order
is tougher than ever."

Chuck nodded his head and listened intently, his eyes roaming the countryside for animals in the meantime.

"But that doesn't change the fact that the jobs open for my people are jobs like elevator operators or porters or chauffeurs or a job like mine with Masterson—a sort of personal valet."

Arthur paused, seeming to grope for a thought, struggling to give tongue to it. "It's a new form of slavery, Chuck, and you sort of grow used to the yoke, forgetting what freedom—real freedom—is really like. Masterson paid me a good salary, but he was paying for my soul." He turned his head toward Chuck and smiled a timid smile. "I've got my soul back now, Chuck. It feels good."

"A long time ago, a man named Stephen Vincent Benet . . ." Chuck started.

"*The Devil and Daniel Webster,*" Arthur said, nodding. "I read that when I was very young. All about a man who sells his soul to the devil. He got his soul back, too, as I recall."

"Yes," Chuck said. "He did."

They fell silent, walking side by side, the primitive world spreading around them in lush greenness. They didn't say another word until much later when Chuck called a halt for an early supper.

He watched their faces as they ate, huddled around the fire Pete had built. He tried to read expressions, tried to fathom what was going on behind the masks. It might be important, he knew. They had a long journey ahead. He had to know which of the party he could count on and which he couldn't trust. His

eyes moved from one face to the next, and his mind
made its silent calculations.

Masterson: He didn't know. He could read nothing
there, nothing at all. The man's eyes were veiled, and
his mouth was expressionless. He only knew that this
was the man who had killed Owen and he automatically distrusted him. He wanted to believe that
the man was simply ignorant, but he sensed something deeper behind Masterson's actions. What that
something was, he could not tell. Masterson's face
gave no clue.

Denise: She sat by the fire drinking a cup of warm
broth. The light danced in her hair, igniting it with
flashing sparks. Her brown eyes had somehow lost
their luster, and there were tired lines stretching from
the wings of her nose to her lips. Chuck felt that
Denise was repulsed by her uncle's behavior. But he
was still her uncle, and he wondered how far her
allegiance would stretch when the cards were down.
He knew for certain that the rigors of the journey
were leaving their mark on her. She no longer walked
with a spring in her step. There was a weary slump
to her shoulders. He would have to watch her carefully. The country could be very hard on a girl.

Arthur: He squatted on his haunches by the fire,
a big, powerful brown man. There was a peaceful
expression on his face as he sipped at his coffee, an
expression of mild contentment. Arthur could be
trusted. Yes, Chuck would trust him with his very
life.

Pete: Chuck felt he could trust him, too. But somehow, he wasn't sure. The cook's main interest was

cooking, true. But until Chuck knew what Masterson's
stake in all this was, he could not be sure where Pete's
real interests lay. He began to regret the fact that he
had armed the jovial-looking cook. Uneasily, he wondered how he could reclaim the rifle without insulting
the man.

Gardel: If anything, he was even more dangerous
than Masterson. In the days of the racketeers, Gardel
would have been a hired gun, a man who killed for
money. This was Chuck's impression. There was
craftiness in the thin man's eyes, a craftiness that
carried down to the tilt of his mouth and the set of
his jaw. If Masterson gave the word, Gardel would
obey it. And with Masterson giving the word, there
was no telling what might happen.

Chuck added these impressions mentally. There
was one person he was sure of, two on the borderline
and two he definitely did not trust. It didn't sound
good.

He was suddenly aware of the hum of conversation around him. He picked up his plate and picked
at the vegetables on it, listening to the voices.

"And I say," Pete was arguing, "that Man wouldn't
have stood a chance if he appeared on earth the same
time these reptiles were running around. They'd have
gobbled him up in the space of a week, and that
would have been the end of the human race."

"There's no way of knowing," Arthur said. "The
big reptiles had already died out before Man
appeared. Isn't that right, Chuck?"

"Yes," Chuck answered. "Long before Man appeared."

"Well, I'm just saying for the sake of argument," Pete said.

"There are too many 'ifs,' " Arthur answered. "Man may have survived in spite of the reptiles."

"I doubt that strongly," Masterson said suddenly.

"Why?"

"Primitive man was an extremely ignorant animal. The cave man was very close to the ape. Can you picture an ape in combat with one of these monsters?"

"An ape doesn't have Man's intelligence," Arthur said.

"*Modern* man's intelligence," Masterson corrected. "The *cave* man was not intelligent."

"He discovered fire," Arthur said. "And he learned to make tools and to domesticate animals and to decorate his caves, and . . ."

"I dislike arguing with you," Masterson said, spreading his palm wide. "You don't know what the deuce you're talking about!"

Arthur got to his feet and a wild light danced in his eyes. "Masterson . . ." he started, and then Pete yelled.

"A cave man!"

For a second Chuck thought Pete had taken Masterson's side and was throwing a slur at Arthur. One look at the cook, though, told him he had been mistaken. Pete was standing on his feet, his eyes wide with shock, his face pale against his splotchy freckles. One arm was outstretched, and the pointing finger trembled as it stabbed the air, indicating a fringe-covered outcropping of high rocks.

"A cave man," he repeated, his voice excited. "I

saw one. I saw one. Over there. On the rocks." He
unslung his rifle and pulled back the bolt.

Chuck leaped to his feet instantly, putting his hand
on Pete's arm. He could feel the man still trembling.

"Take it easy," he said. "You're letting all this talk
get you. There are no cave men in Jurassic times."

"I saw one," Pete insisted. "A shaggy man with a
beard, and . . . and hairy legs. Right on top of those
rocks."

"That's impossible," Chuck said mildly.

"Maybe it ain't so impossible," Gardel put in.
"Maybe the scientists are all wet. Maybe there are
cave men in these times."

"Come on," Chuck shouted to Pete. He began running toward the rocks, the cook close behind him.

"Be careful!" Arthur shouted.

Chuck nodded, and he felt his heart start its in-
fernal thumping against his ribs again.

Deliberately, he slid the .45 from its holster at his
waist and gripped the walnut stock tightly.

Chapter 9 Encounter

H E did not for an instant believe that Pete had seen
a cave man. Chuck had too much respect for
science to believe that its theories could have been
so grossly inaccurate. He did not doubt, however,
that Pete had seen a man. Pete's eyes were certainly
as good as anyone's, and he could tell a man from a
dinosaur the same way anyone else could in broad
daylight. He was not too happy about Pete's discovery, though.

"He went this way," Pete said, breathing hard alongside Chuck. "See his tracks?"

Chuck nodded, making his way through the foliage,
his palm sweating against the gun butt.

Tempomaniac.

The word popped into Chuck's mind, and he could
not dislodge it. Tempomaniacs were dangerous people. They were the borderline schizophrenics of his
own time. Instead of leaping all the way into the

97

nontrespassable reaches of insanity, they chose escape
in another form. When the demands of society became too great, they left society, seeking refuge and
asylum in the uncluttered past. Tempomania was a
serious criminal offense. The offender could not plead
complete insanity because there were tests that would
immediately establish his normality. And the government *had* to be strict with offenders. The entire balance of the present could be seriously thrown out of
whack by these marauders into the past.

A tempomaniac confronted with capture, therefore, was almost like a cornered wild animal. If this
man Pete had seen turned out to be a tempo . . .
Chuck shuddered at the thought.

"There he goes!" Pete shouted.

Chuck looked up instantly, and this time he saw
the man, too. He was built heavily, with shaggy brown
hair and a flowing brown beard. He turned for a
moment, and his eyes glared fiercely in his frightened,
pale face.

"Stop!" Chuck shouted.

The man turned and fled, scrambling over the
rocks like a frightened creature of the woods. His
fingers scrabbled wildly, and he pushed himself upward, almost on all fours. The face of the outcropping was dotted with small, tunnel-like caves. The
man climbed the sheer, angled rock with practiced
skill, darting into one of the deep holes in its face.

"He went into one of the caves," Pete said. He was
holding the rifle tightly in his hands, and his mouth
was drawn across his face in a tight line.

"I think he's a tempo," Chuck said tersely.

Pete sounded disappointed. "Not a cave man?"

"No. There's no such thing in Jurassic times, Pete."

"A tempo, huh? That's not so good."

"No. In fact, it's bad."

"What are we going to do?"

"We'll have to try to take him."

"Why?"

Chuck turned to Pete in surprise. "What do you mean, *why?*"

"Why not leave him here? I'm not anxious to meet my Maker, Chuck."

"He's a criminal," Chuck said firmly. "If we left him here, we'd be helping him."

Pete seemed to consider this for a moment. "I hadn't looked at it that way," he said.

"Are you with me then?"

"I'm with you. What's our next move?"

"Let's get closer to the cave."

Together, almost like reptiles themselves, they crawled on their bellies until they were only several feet away from the mouth of the cave. There they lay flat on the angular rock.

"What now?" Pete whispered.

For answer, Chuck lifted his .45 and fired a shot into the air. The echoes of the shot bounded over the steep rock surface, spread over the land and then died away.

"We know you're in there," Chuck called.

There was no answer. Without hesitation he fired another shot, waiting for the echoes to die before he spoke again.

"You'd better come out," he shouted.

There was another long silence, and then a voice called, "Go away. Go away." The voice sounded tired and desperate.

"Come out, or we'll come in shooting," Chuck answered.

"Go away," the voice said again.

"You heard me," Chuck called. "We'll count to three."

He waited for an answer and when he got none he shouted, "One!" His voice bounced off the rocks, seemed to fill the countless caves that sat like black pockmarks on the face of the outcropping.

"Two!"

Again the echoes and the long silence after the echoes had dissipated themselves over the rocks and the earth.

He was ready to call again when the voice shouted, "Please! Go away. Please!"

"Three!" he shouted.

He waited again and then said, "All right, we're coming in."

He and Pete began crawling closer to the cave, their eyes on the black opening.

"Are we going to shoot?" Pete asked.

Chuck bit his lip. "I don't know. I didn't think he'd call my bluff. I guess . . ."

He saw movement at the cave's entrance and he shut his mouth at once, bringing up the .45. The man they had chased appeared in the opening, his hands over his head, his eyes blinking at the sunlight.

"Don't shoot," he said. "Don't shoot."

Chuck watched him as he came further from the

cave's mouth, ready to counteract any trick. And
then he saw more movement at the entrance.

"Hold it!" he called.

The man stopped in his tracks.

"Who else is in the cave?" Chuck asked.

"My colleague," the man said.

"Only one other man?"

"Yes, that's all."

"Tell him to come out with his hands up."

The man turned to the cave. "Come out, Pierre,"
he said. "With your hands up. They are armed."

Pete swung his rifle around to cover the first man
while Chuck kept his eyes on the entrance. A small
man stepped out into the sunlight, the strong rays
glancing off the thick eyeglasses on the bridge of
his nose. He was bald, with a broad, flat nose and
thin lips. In contrast to his glistening pate, his chin
and face were covered with a wiry black beard that
lent a ferocious look to his otherwise timid features.
He walked forward slowly, blinking his eyes. When
he saw Chuck, he said, "Why, you're just a boy!"

There was a faint accent to his voice, and Chuck
couldn't place it until he recalled that the first man
had called him Pierre. French. The first man still
stood with his hands over his head, and Chuck had
a good opportunity to look him over more carefully.

He was broad across the shoulders and chest, a
heavily built, squat man, who somehow resembled
a shoe salesman, with a thick furry beard. He had
brown hair and brown eyes and a slightly curving
nose that looped down to a sensitive mouth with a
pouting lower lip.

The second man moved up close to him and said, "He is just a boy, John. A boy with a gun."

"*I* ain't a boy, Mister," Pete said.

The first man looked at Pete and then squared his shoulders. "Now that you have us, what are you going to do with us?"

His voice was cultured, an educated voice with the ring of authority behind it. Chuck stared at the man, trying to analyze the peculiar quirks of character that made men seek escape into the past.

"I don't know exactly," Chuck said. "Take you back, I suppose."

"Take us back where?" the second man wanted to know.

"Why, to the authorities, of course."

"The *what?*"

"The authorities," Chuck repeated, tightening his grip on the .45.

The bigger man started to laugh. "Please," he said, "don't overtax our credulity."

"I don't understand you," Chuck said. He was beginning to feel nervous. Something was all wrong.

"Why would a tempomaniac take us to the authorities?" the man asked, a smile on his face.

"*What?*"

"We know you're tempos," the little man with the glasses said. "There is no need to pretend."

"How do you like that?" Pete said, incredulity stretching his face. "They're calling *us* tempos!"

"We're on a chartered time slip," Chuck said, his voice firm. "We're taking you back to . . ."

The big man dropped his arms and took a step toward Chuck, his face erupting in a beaming smile.

"Stay where you are!" Pete snapped.

"But this is wonderful," the spectacled man shouted. "John, do you realize what this is? These people . . ."

"Hold it, hold it," Pete said.

"What's this all about?" Chuck wanted to know.

The spectacled man stepped forward, lowering his hands. "Let me introduce myself. I am Dr. Pierre Dumar, a geologist. This," and here he indicated the bigger man, "is Dr. John Perry, a paleontologist."

"What?"

"Exactly," the big man said. "Why, we thought you were tempos!"

"And we thought *you* were tempos," Chuck said, the humor of the situation beginning to dawn on him.

"Be careful," Pete said warily, "this may be a trick."

"No, no," Dr. Dumar assured him. "Here. Here are my papers." He reached into the back pocket of his tattered trousers and pulled out a leather billfold. While he rummaged in one of the compartments, he said, "John, show the boy your papers."

Dr. Perry reached into his pocket, and Pete raised his rifle expectantly. Dr. Dumar extended a celluloid case, and Chuck looked at it with scrutiny. He saw the seal of the United States Government and under that the hourglass seal of the Department of Chronology.

"It's all right, Pete," he said. "Put up your rifle."

He holstered the .45 and offered his hand to Dr. Perry. The paleontologist took it and squeezed it firmly. "Are we delighted to see you!" he said. "We've been lost for close to six months now."

Dr. Dumar put his billfold back into his trousers pocket and his pale blue eyes sparkled behind the

thick lenses of his glasses. "We've been searching for
the rendezvous site," he explained. "You see, we were
granted a scientific dispensation to study the period.
Our grant expired six months ago, at which time we
were to be at the rendezvous site for a slip back to
the present." He shrugged his shoulders helplessly.
"We couldn't *find* it! We have been over this ground
a thousand times, but we cannot find the area."

"Before you raise your hopes," Chuck said, "we
don't know where the site is, either."

"Oh?" Dr. Perry raised his eyebrows.

"We've had a series of accidents," Chuck said. The
memory of Owen suddenly focused sharply in his
mind. He stopped talking, nursing the ache in his
heart.

Pete seemed to warm up suddenly. "We're looking
for the site now," he said. "You're welcome to join
us."

Dr. Dumar nodded. "The four of us should be
able to . . ."

"There's more than four of us," Pete said. "We've
got another four people back at our camp."

"All the better," Dr. Perry put in. "Our chances
should increase with our numbers. This is a vigorous
land."

Dr. Dumar nodded. "We have been living off the
countryside for the past four months. Foraging. It
has not been pleasant."

"Let's get started," Chuck said. "You'll want to
meet the rest of the party. And Pete will rustle up
some grub for you. He's our cook."

Dr. Perry smiled, his teeth glistening against the

darkness of his beard. "An excellent fellow to know," he said.

They started toward the camp, and a new worry began to gnaw at Chuck's mind. They had been forced to take along a meager supply of food as it was— and now there were two extra mouths to feed!

He sighed deeply, convinced that they would never again see their own time, that they would remain among the reptiles forever.

Chapter 10 Water to Cross

THE camp was silent when they returned. Masterson and Gardel were seated on a low rock, their heads bent together as they spoke in low whispers. They stopped talking when Chuck appeared. Arthur and Denise were squatting by the fire, one of Denise's long, blue-jeaned legs stretched out toward the warmth of the crackling flames.

When Arthur saw Chuck, he leaped to his feet and brought his rifle up, his eyes swinging to the two strangers.

"Relax, Arthur," Chuck said easily. "They're friends." He led the two doctors to the fire and said, "Dr. Dumar and Dr. Perry, this is the rest of our party. The fellow behind the gun is Arthur."

"Pleased to know you," Arthur said. He extended his hand, and both doctors shook it in turn. "I was just about ready to come after you," he said, turning to Chuck. "All that talk about cave men . . ."

"The doctors are far from cave men," Chuck said, smiling. "Dr. Dumar is a geologist, and Dr. Perry is a paleontologist. They were doing some work in the area and couldn't find the rendezvous site when it was time to return."

Masterson walked over to the fire and extended his hand to Dr. Dumar. "Allow me to introduce myself," he said. "I'm Dirk Masterson." He paused and added, "I financed this little expedition."

"Oh!" Dr. Dumar said. A frown started near his bald pate and moved down his forehead to curl his heavy black brows. Then he shook his head and said, "Forgive me. I must have had a mistaken impression."

"About what?" Masterson asked.

"No, nothing. It is nothing. Forgive me."

"I'm interested now," Masterson said, his teeth flashing in an easy grin. His voice had lost all its bluster and was gently insistent now.

"Well," Dr. Dumar said, "I was under the impression that private time slips were restricted to an area immediately surrounding the rendezvous site. I must have been mistaken."

The smile flickered on Masterson's face for an instant, seemed almost to extinguish. It came back stronger than ever, dazzling in its brilliance, and he said, "We had an accident. Our jeep crashed into the force field and shorted it."

Dr. Dumar nodded. "I see. But shouldn't you have remained in the area of the ren . . ."

"This is my assistant, Brock Gardel," Masterson said quickly.

Dr. Dumar smiled. "How do you do?"

Brock shook hands with the geologist and then

turned to Dr. Perry. "You must have had a rough time, all alone back here. How long have you been lost?"

"About six months," Dr. Perry said. His brown eyes studied Gardel as if he had discovered a new form of life for research.

"What brought you here in the first place?" Gardel asked.

Dr. Perry smiled. "The Time Slip, of course."

For a moment Gardel's face went blank with surprise. "Oh," he said. "Oh! Heh heh. Of course. I mean . . ."

"Brock was just wondering if you are the two lost scientists the newspapers have been saying so much about lately," Masterson interceded.

Dr. Perry shrugged. "We haven't seen a newspaper since we left our own time, eight months ago. What have they been saying?"

Masterson shrugged. "Something about your coming back here to map out a large vein of uranium you discovered on a previous expedition."

Dr. Perry's eyes met Dr. Dumar's for an instant. He nodded slowly, then said, "Yes, that's correct. As far as I know, our reason for being here is no secret. Sometime last year Dr. Dumar and I stumbled onto a fantastically wealthy uranium deposit in the course of our roamings throughout Jurassic times. We reported this to the government, and they sent us back again to map out the area. That's what we were doing when we lost our way."

"I see," Masterson said. "The government planned to do a little mining, then?"

"I imagine so," Dr. Perry said. "That, too, is no secret. We need all the uranium we can get. Constructive atomic power has a long way to go yet. We can help it get there if we can supply the needed uranium."

"Where is this huge deposit?" Masterson asked.

Dr. Perry smiled. "That, I'm afraid, *is* a secret."

"Oh, *really*," Masterson said, his eyebrow shooting up onto his forehead.

"My colleague does not wish to sound like a spy in a melodrama," Dr. Dumar interrupted. "But the location of the deposit is a secret. Until the government decides what to do with it, at any rate."

Masterson nodded appreciatively. "Then you have mapped the area?"

"Yes, certainly."

"Well," he said, "it's a lucky thing we stumbled onto you. You might have been lost here forever with all that valuable information on you."

"Yes," Dr. Dumar agreed. "I think we were very lucky to have found you. We have been living off the land, eating small reptiles and . . ."

"Say," Pete interrupted, "how about some hot soup and sandwiches?"

"That sounds like an excellent suggestion," Dr. Dumar said, nodding his bald head.

"In fact," Dr. Perry added, "it's the best suggestion I've heard in the past six months."

Masterson smiled, immediately assuming the role of the benevolent host. "Eat all you like," he said, "and after that we'll get you back to the rendezvous site. Don't worry."

"I hate to be a wet blanket," Chuck said to the

doctors, "but I hope you're not forgetting that we don't know where the site is, either. I think you'd better have a quick meal. Then we'd better get started. It may take us longer to find than you think."

"A sensible suggestion," Dr. Perry said. "Come, Pierre, let's sample some of that soup."

The doctors moved over to the fire, and Masterson went with them, still playing the host, talking and laughing easily with them. Chuck wondered at his sudden change of mood and then shrugged the man off as being completely insane. He had undoubtedly forgotten all about the accident that had taken Owen's life—had forgotten completely that he had indirectly caused the accident. Chuck hadn't forgotten. He thought about it again and wondered why he referred to it as an accident. He recognized it for what it was, of course. A deliberate sacrifice on Owen's part—a move to save his brother and Masterson. But if Masterson hadn't driven the jeep away from the party, if he hadn't frozen at the wheel in the face of the charging brontosaurs . . . Chuck shook his head. There was no point in thinking this way. Masterson *had* deserted the party and he *had* frozen to the wheel—and Owen was dead. For a desperate moment, Chuck wished that he had a portable Time Slip of his own, a mechanism that would allow him to go back over the hours and relive the whole terrible incident. Had he known beforehand . . . He wondered. Would he have left Masterson to die? Or would he have followed the same course of action, automatically rushing to Masterson's rescue, in spite of the impending danger? With Owen's life at stake, Chuck knew what he would have done. Or did he?

If someone came to you and said, "This morning, on the way to school, you will see a man about to be run down by a truck. If you save this man, someone dear to you will be very seriously hurt. If you let him die, you and your loved one will escape without injury," what would you do? You would probably leave the man to die. Or would you save him anyway, thinking that the future would take care of itself—that you might be able to prevent the injury to your loved one even if . . .

The *future!*

Chuck went pale.

The future. What of the future? A spasm of disbelief worked its way through his body. His mind reeled as the full importance of Owen's death registered on his numbed senses.

He tried to shove the realization aside, but it persisted, filling his mind with thoughts that started him trembling again.

Owen had died 100 million years before he had been born!

That meant that Owen had never really existed at all. It meant that back in his own time, devastating changes would be taking place. He could only begin to guess at the smallest of these changes, and they assailed his confused mind like a lethal shower of bullets.

His room. There would only be one bed in the room. Owen's bed would not be there, because Owen had never existed. Owen's books would be gone, his college pennants, his fraternity mug, his desk and his graduation pictures.

Owen's toothbrush would not hang on the rack in the bathroom. Owen's old bicycle would no longer be in the basement. Chuck's mother and father would have had only one son: Chuck.

The idea was staggering in its concept. It meant that all of Owen's records, his school records, his employment records, everything automatically ceased to exist the moment Owen was killed. It meant that his mother and father, his friends, anyone who had ever been influenced by Owen, would automatically have a portion of their personalities changed—the portion Owen had influenced for good or for bad.

But Owen *had* existed. Chuck had grown up with his brother, had . . . had . . .

He shook his head, his mental confusion almost a physical thing.

"What's the trouble, Chuck?" a gentle voice asked.

He turned almost frantically. "My . . . my brother," he blurted.

Arthur was standing beside him, and a puzzled look crossed his face. "I didn't know you had one," he said. "Is something wrong?"

The shock slapped into Chuck with the force of a trip hammer. He opened his mouth, trying to shape words. "But . . . Owen—my brother—Owen. You know him—Owen." He gripped Arthur's arms and looked up into his face. "You know him!" he practically screamed.

Arthur's face grew more puzzled. "Owen?" He shook his head helplessly. "No, Chuck, I'm sorry. I never met him."

Chuck's fingers tightened on Arthur's arm. "Don't

kid me," he said tightly. "Please don't kid me, Arthur."

Arthur's eyes clouded. "You know I wouldn't Chuck," he said softly.

Chuck whirled rapidly and ran to the fire. "Pete!" he called. "Pete!"

The cook looked up, his green eyes widening. "What is it, Chuck?"

"I . . . I . . . want to talk to you. In private."

Pete's features hovered between a smile and a frown. "Why, sure."

He left the fire, and they walked a few feet away from the doctors and Masterson.

"I want to ask you something about . . . about my brother," Chuck said.

"Your brother?"

"Owen. My brother."

Pete shrugged. "Why sure, Chuck, if you think I can help you. I don't see how . . ."

"You *do* know him then?"

"Who?"

"My brother. Owen."

"No," Pete said, "I don't. But if you think I can help, anyway, I'll be glad to."

"Pete!" Chuck shouted. "You saw him killed by the brontosaurs! You condemned Masterson as a murderer. You . . ."

Pete's face expressed concern. "Chuck, are you . . . do you feel all right?"

"Pete, please. Tell me the truth. Tell me what you saw. Tell me what happened when the brontosaurs charged us."

"Well," Pete paused and ran his hand through his bright red hair. "You led us toward the rocks and then you saw that the animals were following us, so . . ."

"I led you toward the rocks? *I* did?"

"Why, yes. Then, when you saw the animals behind us, you ran for the truck and started herding them away from us. Just about that time, you saw Masterson in the jeep and you drove toward him. You got him out of the jeep just in time. Then you came back to camp. You were pretty sore. You wouldn't talk to Masterson, and then you went out alone to look at the jeep."

"With a shovel!" Chuck said, swallowing hard. "I went out to bury . . ."

"No, Chuck. You didn't have a shovel with you."

"Pete, this is the truth? You're not kidding me?"

"No, Chuck, I'm not kidding you. Why? Has something . . . ?"

Chuck didn't wait for the rest of the sentence. He went back to Arthur and asked, "Why'd you quit Masterson?"

Arthur shrugged. "I just had too much all of a sudden. When I saw how close he came to killing you both in that jeep, I figured I'd had enough."

"And Owen—Owen—" Chuck shook his head, trying to clear it. He stumbled over to where Masterson sat with the two doctors.

"Mr. Masterson," he said, "when you hired a guide for this expedition . . ."

"See here, Spencer," Masterson said, "I hope you're not going to start harping on that accident with the jeep again. We got out of it safe and sound."

"When you hired a guide," Chuck said slowly and evenly, *"whom did you hire?"*

"What? I don't understand you."

"Whom did you hire? Who was it?"

"Why, you, of course." His brows pulled together into a deeply perplexed frown. "What's the matter with you, Spencer?"

"Nothing. I . . . I . . ."

"I didn't like the idea of such a young guide, but they said you knew the area well and—say, are you sure you're all right?"

Chuck staggered away from the fire. It had happened already. Owen had been crossed out, eliminated, just as if he'd never existed. He understood now why the party had turned to him as leader. Their minds had already adjusted to the fact that there had never been an Owen. As far as they were concerned, Chuck had *always* been their guide. It was therefore logical that he should be the one to lead them back to the rendezvous site. Even their memories had adjusted themselves. The incident with the jeep had been nothing more than a very close call. No one had been killed because there had been no Owen as far as they knew.

Owen was gone. He had never been.

And everything around him had adjusted to his absence. Time had made its own repairs.

Chuck shook his head again. If they all . . . he didn't understand. He simply didn't understand. Why had they all forgotten there had ever been a person named Owen, when he still remembered? Was it that he had been closest to Owen, that Owen had had a stronger effect on the development of his personality, had contributed more to his memory? Was it just a matter of time then, until he, too, forgot all about Owen? Would he go on living as if he had never had a brother? Would his mind and his body and his memory eventually make the adjustment? And would it be the same with his parents? When he greeted them again in his own time, would they have completely forgotten Owen? Would a son and a brother be completely erased because of a sacrifice 100 million years in the past?

No!

He didn't want to forget Owen. Owen had existed. Owen was his brother. He clung to those facts as he would cling to his sanity. He shook his head, trying to clear it. There were already things he could not remember about his dead brother. Had Owen's bicycle been red or green? Surely, he should remember something as simple as that. He had seen the bicycle every day, behind the stairs in the basement. It was red, wasn't it? No—no, it was green. He shook his head again. He didn't know.

He wanted to cry. The tears gathered in his eyes and he fought to hold them back. He tried to remember what the name of Owen's fraternity had been, but the Greek letters were blurred in his memory. Alpha Beta Tau? Why couldn't he remember? Owen's porcelain mug had rested on the corner of Owen's desk for as long as Chuck could remember. Epsilon Delta Mu? His brows pulled together. No, not that. But what? *What?*

He was beginning to forget already. He bit his lip

and felt the warm, salty blood flow into his mouth. He
didn't want to forget. He didn't want to . . .

"Well, young man," Dr. Perry said, "we've finished
our lunch and we're ready to move whenever you are."

Chuck glanced up at the paleontologist. "What?
Oh, yes, yes. Of course. I . . ."

"If you don't mind, we'd like to go back to the cave
for our instruments and some other things."

"Not at all," Chuck said.

"We'll only be a few minutes."

A few minutes, Chuck thought. *It had taken only a
few minutes for the brontosaurs to crush Owen into
the earth.*

And in those few minutes a lifetime had been lost.

They traveled until it was dark and then they slept
for the night. In the morning they got an early start,
anxious to find the rendezvous site.

The land was completely unfamiliar. Chuck remembered nothing about it. It was as if the party had been
dropped in the center of the African wilds without a
compass, without a map, without a guide. His mind
wrestled with the problem. He knew that they could
wander around forever, covering the same terrain
over and again, without even knowing it. It all looked
the same. The trees, the rocks, the animals—everything.
It was like watching the same slide slipped in and out
of the viewing screen of the same projector, over and
over and over.

Beneath the pressing need for reaching the rendezvous site in time, another problem pulled and
wrenched at Chuck's mind.

He was forgetting more and more details about Owen's life. He found himself wondering which college Owen had attended. He struggled with his memory for a full half-hour before he was forced to give it up as a bad venture. He tried to remember then what kind of automobile Owen had driven. He knew he had driven a car, and that was the maddening part. He had seen the car every day since Owen had bought it. He had helped his brother wax and polish it, had—in fact—learned to drive with it. He went through the names of every automobile he could think of and then gave up in despair.

It seemed impossible that Owen had been dead only since yesterday afternoon. It seemed even more incredible that they had been in Jurassic times for only three days. It felt more like three years.

But the three days gone meant they had only four days in which to find the site. That wasn't much time. Four days were barely enough time to pronounce the names of some of the reptiles of the period, no less find a site that was as elusive as the fastest of the animals.

Chuck began to wonder if they would *ever* find it.

He confided this to Denise shortly before lunch that day.

"It's like pushing through one of those mazes they give rats to play with," he said. "The rendezvous site is the hunk of cheese at the end of the maze. But the maze is full of blind alleys and dead ends and false leads." He shook his head. "I wonder how many rats every reach the cheese."

"You don't think we'll make it, then?"

"I don't know, Denise. I just don't know. I don't recognize a thing about the country. It all looks the same to me, every inch of it."

Denise sighed heavily, pushing a strand of blonde hair off her forehead. "Do you have any idea at all what you're looking for?"

"Yes. A giant pair of white rocks poking up into the sky. When we spot those, I'll know we're somewhere near the site. Until then, we've just got to keep pushing ahead and hoping we're going in the right direction."

"Twin white rocks," Denise murmured.

"And thank God they're white," Chuck said fervently. "Imagine how hard they'd be to find if they were green!"

Denise laughed, but there was a hollow ring to it.

It was midafternoon when Chuck spotted the lake.

"Arthur!" he called.

"What is it, Chuck?" Arthur answered, as he ran to him quickly.

"That lake. It looks familiar."

"Yeah?" Arthur studied the shimmering surface of the distant lake. "It looks like all the other lakes we've seen," he said.

"Let's get closer to it. It rings a bell, somehow."

They made their way down to the edge of the lake, struggling forward through thick growth that sometimes rose higher than their heads. It was slow, torturous labor. Every muscle of the body was called into play against the tenacious plants. It was impossible to relax for a moment. The land seemed to wage a grim battle against the trespassers, determined to let them know it did not approve of their intrusion. It took them the better part of the afternoon to reach the lake, and Pete started supper as soon as they found a good place to make camp.

"I think we're getting closer," Chuck said. "I think this is the lake we camped by the first day—right after our tussle with the stegosaurs."

"I think you're wrong, Spencer," Masterson said.

"Why?"

"Because I think we've been traveling in the wrong direction ever since we met the doctors, that's why."

"That's no reason. You're saying, 'I think you're wrong because I think you're wrong.' Why do you think so?"

"Call it intuition," Masterson said. "Or just plain sense of direction. I know we're heading in the wrong direction, though. I think we ought to start back from where we met the doctors and take it from there."

Chuck sighed and ran his fingers through his short hair.

"I don't know. Maybe you're right."

He realized abruptly that he was talking to Masterson, talking to him in civil tones. The memory of Owen came back sharply and poignantly, and he felt immensely guilty over having forgotten him so completely. He turned away from Masterson and walked down to the water's edge, staring across the lake.

Was that the way it would be? Would Owen keep fading out of his mind until even the memory was lost? Would he eventually forget that Masterson had caused his brother's death? Could he ever forget that?

Could he ever forget something as big and as obvious as, for example, the two white rocks there across the lake? Would that be the pattern of events? The memory would grow dimmer and dimmer and then it would fade completely until only . . .

Two white rocks!

He started so suddenly that he almost fell into the lake. His eyes opened wide, and he stared across the lake in surprised fascination.

"The rocks!" he shouted, pointing wildly. "The twin rocks! There they are!"

He whirled rapidly and ran back to the party.

"The rocks! Across the lake there. We're not far from the site now. Those rocks are right near it."

"Are you sure?" Arthur asked.

"I'm positive," Chuck said. "I'm positive!" He clapped Arthur on the back. "We're going to make it, Arthur. We're going to make it."

"Oh, that's wonderful," Denise squealed.

"What are we standing around for then?" Pete asked. "Let's eat and turn in early so we can get an early start in the morning."

Chuck looked at the rocks again and then his eyes scanned the surrounding countryside. He was remembering how long it had taken them to get down to the lake's edge. If they tried to cut through the growth again, working their slow way around the entire lake, they might not reach the site in time.

"Geometry," he said suddenly.

Gardel looked up, a frown on his face. "What?"

"Geometry. The shortest distance between two points—and in this case, the fastest. A straight line!"

Dr. Dumar looked at the lake and then asked, "You want to cross it?"

"Exactly! Let's have some supper. Then we'll start building a raft. As soon as that's done, we'll be going on the only recorded Jurassic boat ride."

"It might work," Arthur said. "It just might work."

Chuck looked at the twin white pinnacles again and then murmured so that no one heard him, "It *has* to work."

Chapter 11 Vicious Swimmers

THEY didn't start across the lake the next morning. Chuck was disappointed, but he shoved his disappointment aside and concentrated more ferociously on the task of building the raft. He had hoped they could complete the job the night before, after supper. But he had not taken into consideration two important points: the fact that the raft had to be a very large one in order to hold eight people, and the fact that their only tool was a rather dull ax.

They worked eagerly now, fighting against time, knowing that every minute counted.

By midmorning they were still no more than a quarter of the way finished. Chuck began to doubt the wisdom of deciding on the water route rather than the overland one. He saw gloom settle on the faces of every member of the party as the day wore on. Even Pete, cooking the remarkably modern-looking lobsters

123

and crabs he had caught in the lake, did not look
happy.

They concentrated their efforts on chopping down
the large cycads first. The work was slow and back-
breaking. The ax resembled the kind a boy scout car-
ries in his belt. Chuck longed for a real ax—a lumber-
jack's ax or, at least, a sharp ax.

They took turns. The ax changed hands at least a
dozen times every half-hour. From Chuck to Arthur to
Dr. Perry to Dr. Dumar and then around again—and
around once more. Pete was busily adding to their
food supply from the mollusks and decapods he found
in the lake. Denise did not work because Chuck had
refused her offer to wield the ax. The journey was
really beginning to tell on her, and Chuck knew that
the girl was bone-weary.

Masterson and Gardel refused to lend a hand in
what they called "a fool's venture." Chuck didn't try
to force them. He was too busy working against time.

By noon they had what they felt to be enough felled
trees and they set about the job of lashing them together. The raft not only had to be big, it also had to
be strong enough to carry them across the long lake.
Chuck was not discounting the possibility of meeting
dinosaurs in the water, even though he could not see
any from his position on the shore. The raft had to
be strong enough to take a solid tail swipe or a head-on
collision should they encounter any of the brutes. It
also had to be strong enough to withstand the buffet-
ing of the water.

It was not an easy job.

They used all the rope they had with them and then

they cut vines and lashed these together, intertwining them with the slow patience of a weaver.

By three o'clock, without stopping for lunch, they had finished half the job. Pete left his boiled lobsters to grow cold and lent a much-needed hand on the raft. Denise began working on the vines, twining them together into the necessary lashings. Only Masterson and Gardel insisted they were heading in the wrong direction and adamantly refused to be a party to what they termed Chuck's misdirection.

They all stopped for supper at six-thirty. By this time they were exhausted, and the day was almost gone. Chuck no longer hoped to get the raft in the water before nightfall. His only concern was to finish it in time for an early-morning start. They got to work immediately after supper and worked through until almost midnight, laboring in the light of a huge bonfire.

On the morning of the fifth day they launched their vessel. It was a mild day, the kind of day that made Chuck want to take off his shoes and lie on the shore with the sun strong on his bare chest. That kind of day. The lake reflected a flawless blue sky, opened overhead like a parasol. The ferns dipped gracefully under the mild caress of the breeze. It was a day meant for dreaming, a day that needed a fishing pole and a blade of grass sucked dry between the teeth. It was like the beginning of spring, and it gave Chuck the same feeling because he knew they would have half their problem solved once they crossed the lake.

He watched the shore line recede as the raft nosed out into the water. There was a strange happiness inside him, a happiness that nudged his heart, tempting it to burst open like a blossoming flower.

The raft left a mild wake behind it, wrinkles on the surface of the calm, mirror-like lake. It drifted away from the shore and the men dipped their paddles into the water. The raft reached out to gobble up distance like a hungry tortoise.

It wasn't until they reached the middle of the lake that the currents hit them.

"We're turning!" Masterson shouted. "I told you this was a foolish . . ."

The raft had begun to turn abruptly toward starboard and, as it floundered in the grasp of the strong current, it began to whirl—slowly at first—and then with ever-increasing rapidity. It was like some sort of crazy merry-go-round. It spun dizzily, and Chuck dropped to his belly, clinging to the lashings with grasping fingers.

"Everybody down!" he yelled. He saw the two doctors drop to their knees and reach for the safety of the lashings. Masterson and Gardel were already flat on the deck, holding tightly as the raft gained speed. Arthur staggered for a few seconds, tottering like a drunkard, and then dropped down next to Pete, who had wrapped one fist around a lashing near the end of the raft.

"Denise!" Chuck shouted. "Get . . ."

He watched the girl stagger around the raft, her knees buckling, her hands groping blindly. She stumbled forward, and Chuck struggled to get to his knees, the whirling motion making him sick inside. The raft suddenly shook itself free of the whirlpool, was captured in a cross current that sent it zooming forward in a straight line. Another current caught it and deflected its forward motion, slapping it to one side like a billiard ball.

Chuck was up now, reaching forward for Denise, who fell to her knees and began rolling toward the edge of the raft.

"Denise!"

The currents were enjoying themselves now. They were playing catch with the raft, tossing it back and forth like a beanbag. The raft tilted precariously, and Denise rolled rapidly to the edge. There was a blur of movement, and her long legs flashed in the sun, her hands groping for some kind of grip on the deck.

And then she was over the side! Her blonde head disappeared beneath the water, bobbed to the surface like a yellow cork and was swept away suddenly as the current found a new plaything. In ten seconds flat she was thirty feet from the raft, with the distance widening every second. Chuck ran across the raft, stopped near the edge to kick off his shoes, and then dived into the water.

The water was cold. It closed over his head like an icy tomb. He felt the powerful grip of the current yanking at his legs, saw the blue depths eddying before his eyes. He thrust his arms downward and shoved himself up to the surface. His head broke water and he opened his mouth wide, sucking in a great gulp of air. Far off in the distance, like a speck of sunlight against the water, he saw Denise's golden head.

He reached out with one arm, pulled against the water. His other arm came up over his head, completed the stroke, pulled. Up, over, pull. Up, over, pull. He kept his legs going like powerful pistons, never relaxing his struggle against the current. His arms ached from the strain of fighting the water, and his body was numb with the icy coldness that embraced him, but he kept swimming. He was aware of a jumble of voices back on the raft, but they merged together into a meaningless hum in the background. The voices and the raft were not reality. The only real thing was the water and it had to be fought.

Denise hadn't uttered a sound. She kept her head above water, her arms flailing at the blue surface of the lake, her lips trembling with the cold. Chuck's mouth fell open as he saw her head disappear beneath the surface. He quickened his stroke, saw the blonde hair bob up again, to disappear almost immediately afterward. A few more feet now—a few more feet.

He wanted to quit. Every muscle in his body protested against the strokes he was taking, every nerve fiber screamed shrilly whenever he moved. Denise's head came up for a third time. She opened her mouth, and he saw her eyes wide with terror.

And then she went under again.

He dived immediately, the blue-green curtain closing about him. The water was clear and he saw her drifting down, down, her short hair flowing around her head like seaweed. He lashed out with his arms, feeling the pressure on his eardrums as he went deeper and deeper, swimming rapidly after the descending girl. He reached out with one cold hand, felt the clammy touch of her hair as it contacted his fingers. He closed his hand then, grabbing her hair in a firm grip, lashing out with one arm, kicking his feet frog fashion as he looked to the surface far above him.

The sun laid a pale golden sheen on the surface of the water, almost like a metallic lid to a cool, dim coffin. He kept his eyes on the surface, trying not to think of Denise's weight tugging on his arm, trying to forget the aching shriek of his lungs, the frantic pounding of his heart.

He kept on swimming, and the water seemed to get bluer and then darker and blacker. Sudden fear shot up his spine as the thought of passing out assailed him. His lungs were ready to explode. There was no more air in his body, and the lake began to waver and shimmer before his eyes. He kept his eyes on the layer of sunshine above him, and when his head broke the surface he watched the layer disappear in a filigree splash of gold. He pulled Denise's head to the surface, his eyes opening wide when he saw the color of her face. He gulped at the sweet, clean, fresh air, filling his lungs, resting for only a moment and then striking out for the raft.

"Chuck!"

The voice cut through his senses like a dull-edged knife. It was a long time reaching him.

"Chuck!"

The voice was Arthur's, good old Arthur's. Good old Arthur. Good old buddy back on the raft, waiting to help him aboard, waiting with a blanket, maybe.

The second voice that spoke was not Arthur's.

It was a booming voice that spoke with authority, a voice that cracked ominously and then was still.

It was the voice of a high-powered rifle.

It took a long time for this to penetrate. When it did, Chuck rejected it in confusion. Why were they shooting at him?

The gun went off again, and a geyser of water spouted into the air some three feet to Chuck's left.

"Chuck! Behind you!" This was the voice of Dr. Perry. "An ichthyosaur!"

Ichthyosaur? Chuck's mind yanked the word out of his memory, turned it over so that he could examine it more carefully. *Ichthyosaur? Ichthyosaur? I beg your pardon, sir, but haven't we met before? That is to say, the name's familiar, but the face escapes me. Ichthyosaur. Ichthyosaur.* His memory turned the pages of a book, and the word slowly became a body.

The rifle went off again and again. He didn't look back. He kept towing Denise, keeping her head above water, trying to remember what an ichthyosaur was, and wondering why Dr. Perry was so excited, and wondering also what everyone was shooting at.

Large. Yes, surely an ichthyosaur was large.

The rifle sounded again, closer now as he approached the raft.

A powerfully huge body, 25 to 30 feet long, with four flippers, and it swam through the water by lateral undulations of body and tail. A fish? No, not a fish. Simply a reptile that had adapted itself to the water. A reptile with a sharklike dorsal fin and a powerful tail with two vertical lobes. Enormous eyes set in a three-foot-long head. An elongated snout set with as many as 200 sharp teeth. A conical head and slender, beaklike jaws.

This was *Ichthyosaurus quadricissus.*

With jaws that could tear open the toughest hide of the strongest reptile, and teeth that could rip out the flesh.

A flesh eater, the ichthyosaur.

A flesh eater!

"Behind you, Chuck!" and then the bellow of the
rifle again. He turned his head over his shoulder, saw
the rapier-like jaws, the teeth glinting in the rays of
the sun. Sudden fear covered his body with a clammy
chill. He swallowed hard and heard the rifle erupt
again. The ichthyosaur leaped out of the water, its
deep gray flanks gleaming wetly, its white belly looking cold and hard and uncompromising.

Then a flower blossomed on the belly.

There was the boom of the rifle, and the flower
appeared magically—a brilliant red bloom against
the snow-white flesh. The bloom spread as the fish-
like reptile wrenched violently in midair, great jaws
snapping, the blood spreading until it was washed
away in the water as the ichthyosaur splashed down
beneath the surface.

Then it was all over, Chuck thought. The ichthyosaur was gone, and all he had to do was tow Denise
back to the raft and then relax, with the sun warming
his bones and his muscles.

"Good gravy! Another one!" a voice shouted.

Another one? Chuck thought. *Really another? Not
really another one? Please, please not really.*

The rifles started firing, all of them this time, their
voices ringing with wrathful thunder. A spout of
water leaped into the air on the starboard side of the
raft and then cascaded down in a silvery shower that
revealed a massive brown head. Arthur.

Chuck watched Arthur and then he saw the glint
of the ax clutched in his right hand.

"I'm coming," Arthur shouted. "Hold on, Chuck!"

Chuck took a deep breath and turned his head over his shoulder. Behind him he saw the huge dorsal fin of the ichthyosaur as it sliced through the water, the long jaws snapping in fury, the blood of its slaughtered mate spreading around it in deep red silence.

Chuck pulled Denise closer to him and struck out against the water with his free arm.

Behind him he heard the thrash of the water as the reptile gained on him.

Chapter 12 Earthquake

CHUCK felt strange, as if he had no part in it at all. It was as if the ichthyosaur behind him wasn't really a threat to his life, as if Arthur swimming toward him awkwardly, with the ax poised in his fist, was really an apparition.

He only wanted to reach the raft. He kept swimming. Denise was a dead weight on the end of his arm; Arthur was a dim blob on the water ahead, and the sound of the reptile's gnashing teeth behind him merged with the greater sound of the thunder in his ears.

He swam and he saw Arthur pass him. Then the raft suddenly loomed ahead like a square wooden rug. He reached up with one hand and felt the coarse, splintery surface. A stronger hand closed around his own, and he shook his head weakly, dragging Denise up beside him, wanting them to take her aboard first.

When the weight was lifted from his arms, he felt
marvelously light, light enough to drift up into the
sky, almost weightless. Suddenly he *was* drifting up
to the sky, with strong hands clamped under his armpits. He saw red hairs curling on rounded forearms
and he knew that his benefactor was Pete. He was
lowered gently to the deck of the raft.

"Arti—ficial . . . resp . . ." he gulped, struggling
for breath. "Denise. Artificial respiration."

He saw boots near him and a pair of bare feet. The
lashings of the raft were before his eyes, and beyond
those, the water. And in the water he saw a brown
man raise a powerful arm to ward off the swipe of
swordlike jaws. He saw brown fingers close around
the jaws, saw the other arm come back quickly,
caught the flick of the ax as it came down against
the conical-shaped head of the huge reptile. The arm
came back in a blur of brown, and the ax descended
again. And again. Arthur clung to the twisting jaws,
the water splashing up around him as the reptile
twisted furiously. Blood sprayed into the air as the
ax glinted murderously in the sunlight.

He's going to get killed, Chuck thought. *Arthur is
going to die.*

The blackness came in then, as swift and as sudden as Judgment Day, and Chuck drifted off into a
welcome oblivion.

"He's coming around," the fuzzy voice said.

Chuck kept his eyes closed tightly. There was a
warm orange glow on them, capping them shut,
obliterating everything but its own brilliance.

The voice receded down the length of a long black tunnel. A faint spot of light glowed there, grew larger, larger, until it filled Chuck's consciousness.

There was warmth on his face, and the warmth felt good. He didn't want it to go away. He kept his eyes closed because he thought he was dreaming and he didn't want the dream to end.

His eyelids flickered.

He felt his fingers move involuntarily, and then he blinked his eyes rapidly, opened them and closed them once more.

"Chuck?" the fuzzy voice asked.

He wanted to answer, but somehow he couldn't find his voice. He groped for it, reaching into his throat with a swollen, parched tongue. All he could produce was an unintelligible "ugnhhh."

"Chuck?" the voice repeated. It had lost some of its fur and it sounded a little clearer, a lot closer.

"Yes," he said, surprised to discover that he had a voice, after all.

"This is Pete, Chuck. Are you all right?"

"Fine. I'm fine." He opened his eyes, and the sun splashed into them. He closed them quickly, surprised when the smell of growing things invaded his nostrils.

After awhile he opened his eyes again. He was lying on the ground, the ferns spreading around him in green abundance.

"Denise?" he asked, pushing himself to one elbow, his arm sinking into the soft earth.

"She's all right," Pete said. "It took awhile, but we got her breathing again. She's all right."

Chuck didn't want to ask the next question. "Arthur? Is he . . . did he . . . ?"

He heard a hearty laugh echoing in his ears, and then a deep voice boomed, "Chuck, it'll take more than a little old fish to do me in."

He didn't bother telling Arthur that an ichthyosaur was a reptile and not a fish. Instead, he clasped Arthur's hand firmly, a smile covering his face. "Thanks, Arthur," he said. "Thanks . . . a . . . whole lot."

"Shucks, I enjoyed the swim," Arthur said.

"We made it, I guess." Chuck sat up and looked around him. Far in the distance he saw the twin white rocks leaping up at the sky.

"We made it," Pete repeated. "Once we got rid of those ichthyo-whatever-you-call-'em, the rest was easy."

Chuck looked again at the white rocks. "There's our goal," he said. He paused. "You think we'll get there in time?"

"Why not?" Arthur asked.

"We've only got two days. That's an awful lot of distance to cover in . . ."

"We'll do it," Pete interrupted. "But first I'm going to make some hot chow for you."

"Maybe we ought to get started right . . ."

"Not until you and Denise have eaten," Pete said firmly. Chuck noticed that the cook still carried his rifle slung over his shoulder. He wondered now why he had ever doubted Pete's loyalty. He hugged his knees to his chest as Pete started a fire. Masterson was in animated conversation with the doctors. Gardel was standing off by himself, leisurely puffing on a cigarette. Chuck saw Denise lying on a blanket in the center of the camp. He got up, staggering a little when he discovered his legs weren't as strong as he'd thought, and then walked over to her.

"Hi," he said, "enjoy your morning swim?"

"Oh, delightful," she answered. "Nothing like a swim to give you an appetite."

"Nope, my brother always used to say—" He cut himself short, wondering how he had planned to complete the sentence. For the life of him, he couldn't remember what Owen always used to say. Something about swimming, of course. But what? *What?*

"Do you feel all right, Chuck?"

He snapped his attention back to Denise. "Yes, yes, I'm fine. I hear they really had to tear *you* away from the gates of heaven, though."

"I guess it was all that water I drank," Denise said, laughing lightly. "You see, I prefer orange juice in the morning."

"Of course," Chuck said. "I understand completely."

They both laughed loudly and then stopped short when they heard a loud, raucous voice begin a song.

The saurs I've cooked are bronto,
Stego,
Ptero; but you can keep your Allo,
A heck of a cook is me!
Hi-ho, diddle-ee-oh,
One, two, three!

"Oh no," Chuck moaned. "He's making up his own lyrics now!"

❊   ❊   ❊   ❊   ❊

*I've always been a cook-oh, a cook-oh, that's
me . . .*

But this time, Chuck joined in the chorus.

*Hi-ho, diddle-ee-oh
One, two, three!*

They started out for the twin rocks after Chuck
and Denise had eaten. Dr. Dumar kept running ahead
like an eager cocker spaniel, picking up rocks wherever he found them, carrying a large instrument case
in one hand and his specimens in the other.

Dr. Perry, on the other hand, stayed close to Chuck,
pointing out the various flora and fauna of the period.
On one occasion, when the flurry of wings overhead
announced a visitor, Chuck looked up, fully expect-
ing to see a pterosaur. He was surprised when he
saw one of the most awkward-looking creatures he'd
ever seen in his life.

The animal had distinctive bird features: a beak,
feathered wings, and it was—of course—flying. But
there the resemblance ended, for it also had a very
long tail and the toothed jaws of a reptile.

"That, my friend," Dr. Perry said, "is one of the
first birds. His name is *Archaeopteryx,* the species
macrura."

Chuck shook his head slowly. "It doesn't look very
much like a bird. It looks more like . . . like . . . a
flying squirrel or something."

"No," Dr. Perry said. "Most zoologists agree that
Archaeopteryx was the first bird. It has birdlike feet

and skull, feathered wings and tail, but reptilian teeth. Far removed from the modern bird, of course, but a bird nonetheless."

Chuck looked up at the flying creature and blinked his eyes. "That tail . . ."

"As a matter of fact," Dr. Perry interrupted, "the tail is possibly its most interesting characteristic. In modern birds, the tail proper is shortened to a rudiment ending in a large bone, with the feathers radiating from it to form a tail fan. But take a look at this customer."

His finger pointed up at the bird, tracing its tail as it moved in awkward, flapping flight.

"His tail is as long as the rest of his vertebral column. It consists of twenty-one joints, with the tail feathers in pairs on each side."

"What does it all mean?" Chuck asked.

"It's significant only in that the tail fan of *Archaeopteryx* differs from that of modern birds in exactly the same manner that the tail fins of the earliest fishes differs from that of modern fishes."

"Being vertebrated you mean?"

"Why yes, exactly." Dr. Perry nodded his head appreciatively.

"What does *Archaeopteryx* mean?" Chuck asked.

"It means 'primordial winged creature.' "

"And *macrura?*"

"That simply means 'long-tailed.' "

"A long-tailed, primordial winged creature," Chuck said. "That's quite a mouthful. It's easier to say *Archaeopteryx.*"

Dr. Perry smiled. "Yes, it is." He paused and said,

"Many zoologists felt that the reptilian characteristics dominated and that it should be called a birdlike reptile, rather than a reptilian bird. One thing is certain, though."

"What's that?"

"Birds evolved from reptiles."

"Mmmm."

"But they did not necessarily evolve from pterosaurs or flying reptiles."

"I see," Chuck said.

Dr. Perry smiled again. "You must forgive me for running on like this. I sometimes get carried away and forget that I'm not in front of a classroom giving a lecture."

"I didn't mind at all," Chuck said honestly.

"You're being much too tolerant. You probably know all this, anyway—being a guide, I mean."

"A—guide?"

"Why, yes. That is—well, yes, you are the guide for the expedition, aren't you?"

"My brother . . ." Chuck cut himself short. There was no sense explaining it. No sense telling him how Noah had led the expedition until he'd met his death that day with the brontosaurs. Noah meant nothing to anyone but Chuck now. Noah . . .

A puzzled look crossed Chuck's face. He struck a pensive posture, his face screwed up, his eyes clearly confused. Noah?

"Is anything wrong?" Dr. Perry asked.

Chuck shook his head rapidly. "No, nothing. Nothing at all."

And yet . . . Noah. There was something about

that name. Why, of course. The name wasn't Noah! It was . . . was . . .

Sudden panic fluttered inside Chuck's chest.

What was his brother's name?

Not Noah, surely. Something similar, yes, but not Noah. Something like Aaron . . . or Orrin. . . . No, no, that wasn't it. But what? He felt an aching pain lash through his body, a pain that swept over his mind as he struggled with the memory, trying to dislodge it from its dark corner.

"Are you sure you're all right?" Dr. Perry asked again. "That time you spent in the water . . ."

"I'm all right," Chuck said harshly. He bit down on his tongue then and said, "I'm sorry, Dr. Perry. I just . . . I . . ."

"You probably feel weak, owing to the time . . ."

"*Owen!*" Chuck shouted aloud, relief washing over his mind. "Owen!"

Dr. Perry stared at him curiously. "I don't understand," he said.

"Never mind, Dr. Perry," Chuck answered. "But thanks a lot. Something you said reminded me of something I'd . . . something I'd almost . . ." He swallowed. The word was difficult to say. ". . . forgotten."

But he hadn't forgotten. He still remembered. Owen wasn't even a memory to the others who had known him, but Chuck would never forget. *Never*, he promised himself. *Never!*

He set his lips firmly, his eyes on the white rocks in the distance.

❋ ❋ ❋ ❋ ❋

The terrain got rougher as they moved along.

The twin rocks dangled before their eyes like a promised present. They didn't seem to get any closer. The rocks stood on the horizon like two disdainful monarchs surveying their domain, a king and a queen with proud, cold bearing.

The plants were an army fighting for their monarchs. They threw themselves in the path of the invaders, erecting a wall of living, writhing greenness that held the line with remarkable tenacity. And the monarchs had strewn the path with booby traps; deep mud pits, sharp rocks, wide clefts in the earth, rock faults and slips, sliding talus.

The party waged a war against the country. Arthur was the forward guard, wielding the ax with a powerful arm that felled the foe. Pete was behind him with a meat cleaver, hacking at the tenacious plants. The rest of the party followed behind them, exhausted and ready to call it a day.

And over it all, constantly nagging, was Masterson. He whined interminably, telling them they'd taken the wrong path, that they'd struck out in the wrong direction after they met the lost scientists. Chuck tried to close his ears against the verbal barrage, trusting his memory of the rocks over the guesswork of Masterson.

He was not at all sure they would reach the rendezvous site in time. Nor was he sure that the party would get there safely. Arthur had been forced to shoot and kill two flesh eaters that had boldly attacked the group in a small clearing. It had been simple to kill them. They were small and their hides couldn't very well stop a steel-jacketed bullet.

But Chuck kept thinking of *Allosaurus* wondering what the outcome would be if they ran across this dreaded flesh eater. He crossed his fingers, thankful that they had not seen any of these gigantic carnivores as yet. But could their luck last forever? And what good would a puny rifle be then? He thought of the enormous monster with its razor-sharp teeth and slashing claws, and a shiver wormed its way up his spine.

The sky behind the twin rocks turned a bright red as the sun dipped below the horizon. The red shifted color, shot with purples and oranges, deepening rapidly. And then the dusk hurried quietly across the sky. Night came, enfolding the land in an inky black cloak. The white rocks showed dimly in the darkness, with the stars wheeling sharply overhead like bitter white beaks pecking at the blackness.

Chuck called a halt for the night, aware that tomorrow was the sixth day and that time was running out swiftly. He debated the prospect of going on all night, but one look at Denise's exhausted condition told him they ought to stop for much-needed sleep.

Pete put together a fast, delicious supper, and the party turned in. No one needed coaxing. They crawled wearily into their blankets and were asleep almost before they were fully stretched out.

Chuck took the first watch, telling Arthur he'd wake him in two hours.

He stood by the fire, listening to the familiar crackle of the logs. The wood sputtered and hissed with its newness, and Chuck thought of autumn fires in his own century, with the woods blanketed in

yellow and red leaves, and the air knifed with the
tang of approaching winter. He thought of Halloween
and juicy red apples, crisp and cold to the palate,
sharp against the teeth. He thought of his brother
smoking a pipe on their long walks through the
woods, with the leaves shifting and rasping underfoot, with nature dressed in a pretty party frock. He
thought of pork roasting on an outdoor grill, with
the fat dripping into the fire, the flames leaping with
each fallen drop and the tangy aroma of the meat
flooding the cold, clear air. He could almost feel the
touch of a tweed collar against the back of his neck,
the friendly, rough warmth it gave, and the clothy
smell of the coat when it was taken out of the closet
after a long seasonal rest. There was always a bitter-
sweetness about autumn—the memory of a summer
dying, the cast-iron skies overhead forecasting the
approaching winter. He thought of home now, and
an overwhelming nostalgia swept over him. Familiar
things and places, familiar faces. His own time. Home.

He was deep in his thoughts.

So deep that the ground beneath his feet was
trembling violently before he realized anything was
wrong.

Chapter 13 No Sign

A T first he thought he had fallen asleep and was
dreaming. Then he looked down at the ground,
and his heart leaped into his mouth. Three feet
from where he was standing, the ground was tearing apart in a wide slit that opened like a grinning
mouth.

He started to move just as the land beneath his
feet jerked violently into the air, knocking him to
his knees. He struggled to his feet again, tottering on
the brink of the chasm that was opening wide before
him. Without looking down into the cleft, he leaped
across it, falling to his knees on the other side.

"Wake up!" he shouted. He yanked back the bolt on
his rifle, slammed it home and triggered a shot into
the air. He knew what was happening now, all right.
He knew only too well. He clambered to his feet
again, was knocked down almost instantly as the

145

ground writhed convulsively. "Wake up!" he bellowed, and he heard Arthur boom, "What in
blazes . . ."

Masterson was awake now, and Chuck heard his
raucous voice shout, "Good gravy! An earthquake!"

Then the voices of other members of the party
joined the chorus, voices that had sprung from throats
tight with the snugness of sleep. It was dark, and
darkness always adds confusion—and fear. Not that
darkness was necessary; anyone waking from a sound
sleep to find the ground shivering beneath him would
be confused and frightened. Add to that the fact
that the party was in a strange time, in what was
virtually a strange land, and the result was chaos.

Chuck stumbled forward, the ground leaping under
his feet.

"Chuck!" Dr. Perry shouted.

Chuck recognized the voice in the darkness. He
groped forward, trying to locate the paleontologist.

"Here, Chuck. Here."

In his haste he almost knocked the doctor over.
Dr. Perry gripped Chuck's shoulder and said, "An
upheaval, Chuck, not at all uncommon in these times.
Ever run across one?"

"No, sir. I . . ." His sentence was strangled in
his throat as the ground slammed up against his
feet, knocking him off balance. From out of nowhere,
Dr. Dumar was suddenly standing beside him. The
little Frenchman's voice was strangely soft, mildly
accented.

"Chuck, we have to get out of here at once. These
upheavals are very bad, very bad. The earth will be

bending in upon itself, folding over, opening, slipping. It may be only a local upheaval, so let us try to get away from it."

"All right," Chuck said. He swallowed the lump in his throat. "Everybody here? Better sound off!"

There was a brief lull. For a moment Chuck thought the upheaval was exhausted. In the silence, the voices of the party sounded strangely loud.

"Arthur here."

"Pete here."

"Masterson."

"Gardel."

"Dr. Perry."

"Dr. Dumar."

Chuck waited. The silence hugged the earth tightly. It was an ominous silence, deathly still, forbidding,

"Where's Denise?" he asked.

Again the silence.

Chuck's voice rose, almost breaking. "Where's Denise?"

"She was sleeping near . . ." Pete never had a chance to finish his sentence. The entire party was suddenly knocked over like a batch of bowling pins. Chuck felt himself sail into the air, the rifle clutched tightly in one hand, his other hand reaching out for the ground as he came down heavily. He landed solidly, and then the ground threw him into the air again—and everything seemed to come apart at the seams.

He wanted to run.

His first reaction was a blind, unreasoning one bred of terror. *Run*, his mind screamed, *run, run, run!*

He saw figures bouncing off the ground like drunken marionettes, saw a tremendous portion of the land suddenly slide away from another portion, jutting up into the air. It rose rapidly, like a solid rock elevator, its sides screaming shrilly as rock rubbed rock.

"Denise!" Chuck shouted. "Where are you?"

From the top of the faulted rock, now jutting up some ten feet in the air, he saw Pete scramble to his feet and leap off the edge to the ferns below. He landed with a resounding *thud,* and Chuck was starting for him when the ground behind him suddenly folded over like a newspaper. He saw layers of rock twisting like rubber, saw cycads torn from their section of earth, their roots bared and pleading, like so many tormented fingers. He lost sight of Pete, saw Masterson dart before the path of a falling evergreen and lose himself as the tree crashed to earth. The ground opened then, swallowing the tree, swallowing the spot that Masterson had occupied a few moments before.

There were new sounds now, noises that grew in volume, joining with the grating thrash of the rocks and the earth, mingling with the thunder of the upheaval to form a new kind of chaos—a screaming, shrieking, bellowing bedlam. The animals!

Chuck wanted to stuff his fingers into his ears. He wanted to scream. He wanted to die. He kept running and shouting, "Denise, Denise!"

His feet were off the ground more than they were on it. He shivered involuntarily as the reptiles slithered past, their jaws wide, their eyes opened in blind fright, their throats throbbing with inhuman screeches.

"This way, Chuck," a familiar voice called. He
recognized it as Arthur's and he turned toward it.
He caught a glimpse of Arthur, and then a large
reptile ran past, its long legs thumping the ground,
its forelegs tucked against its chest, looking ridiculously like a rabbit munching a piece of lettuce. The
jaws opened and closed spasmodically on nothing
but air. But when the creature had passed, Arthur
was gone.

Now there were more animals. They seemed to
come out of the very bowels of the earth. They
covered the land, slithering, flying, running on their
hind legs, thundering over the ground on all fours.
They came in pairs or alone or in large herds. They
swarmed over the ground, being swallowed by the
earth, being crushed beneath tons of folding and falling rock. They leaped over trees, butted them aside,
snapped viciously at the foliage.

They screamed or they roared or they squeaked
or they were silent. But they were all terrified, and
the terror gave them speed, but it also made them
blind.

"Chuck!" It was Arthur's voice again. This time
Chuck ran toward it instinctively. He felt a large
hand close over his own and he was yanked toward
a large evergreen as the ground behind him opened
with a low grumble.

"Thanks," he murmured.

"Some fun," Arthur said. "Nothing like a little rock-
slide, I always say."

"Watch out!" Chuck shouted.

A stegosaur shoved its way through the ferns, up-
rooted a cycad, thundered past, its hard armor pass-

ing within two feet of them. Arthur let out a deep sigh, and Chuck echoed it.

"Where are the rest?" he asked.

"I don't know. We'll have to wait until this calms down a little, I guess. Where do you suppose . . ."

A loud rumble filled the air, and Arthur and Chuck began to run. They had come to recognize the sounds already. They had no sooner cleared the spot they'd been standing on when the ground twisted upward, doubling over itself, leaving a strange, warped hump in the air.

"Look!" Chuck said.

It was Pete. He leaped across a chasm in the earth, dodged the swoop of a frightened pterosaur and ran for them quickly. His clothes were in shreds. He was carrying what looked like a sack of empty clothes in his arms. He came closer. The bundle in his arms took on form, became more than a blurred outline.

"Denise!" Chuck exclaimed. "He's got Denise!"

Pete staggered forward, running with the animals, side-stepping the falling trees and the hurtling rocks.

"Hey!" he shouted.

"This way, Pete!"

He was with them in another moment. His face was flushed, and his breath was uneven and ragged.

"She was out like a light," he said. "The first jolt must have knocked her unconscious. I found her right where she'd been sleeping." He shook his head wearily. "Brother, this is some mess, ain't it?"

"We'd better get moving," Chuck said. He looked at Denise's pale face, the moon lighting it wanly, and a pang of anxiety tugged at his body.

"I think it's letting up," Arthur said suddenly.

"Huh? What?"

"Listen," he whispered.

They fell silent, listening to the earth rumble softly. The only sound was the sound of the reptiles, still rushing forward in frantic flight. The bigger noises were gone, though. The earth was at rest again.

After a little while, even the noises of the reptiles died out. The land was as silent as a city street after a sudden summer storm.

They found Dr. Dumar sitting on a low rock, his head cradled in his hands. Tears had dried on his cheeks, and he was shaking his head from side to side when they came up to him.

"My specimens," he said. "All gone. And my instruments."

He kept shaking his head, and Chuck knew that a weaker man would have cracked under the strain of what the doctor had just been through. In a way, he was thankful that Denise had been unconscious throughout the ordeal. He looked at her now, still limp in Pete's arms. "Doc," he said, "see if you can revive Denise, won't you? We want to find the rest of the party."

Dr. Dumar nodded, sighed, and then got to his feet as Pete lowered the girl to the ground. Chuck smiled as he saw the doctor rubbing the unconscious Denise's wrists and then started off with Arthur.

"Do you think he'll be all right?" Arthur asked.

"He's got something to do now," Chuck said. "It'll take his mind off his own troubles."

They moved forward slowly in the darkness. The moon lighted the new landscape, casting a wan yellowness over the twisted trees and the sharply jutting rocks. Chuck could see plainly now, and his eyes carried shocked impressions of the torn land to his brain. He knew that upheavals such as this one, swift and violent, were common occurrences throughout geologic time. He wondered how Man had survived such earthquakes and then he wondered if any upheavals had taken place after Man evolved on earth. He grinned in the darkness. They had survived, hadn't they? A short disturbance, true, but a particularly vicious one—and at least five members of the party had come through it all right.

What of the rest?

Dr. Perry, Masterson and Gardel.

He wanted very much to find Dr. Perry. As for Masterson and Gardel, he didn't much care.

"That's funny," he said aloud.

"Huh?" Arthur asked. "What's funny?"

Chuck faltered. "I . . . I don't know."

Arthur remained silent, his face puzzled.

"I mean," Chuck said, "I'm not sure why I . . . why I . . ."

"Why you *what?*"

"Why I dislike Masterson and Gardel. I just . . . just feel that I do. I mean, aside from all their griping and unco-operativeness. Something deeper. A real dislike. And yet, I have no real reason for it. That is . . ."

"They're not hard to dislike," Arthur said solemnly. "And they've certainly given you enough reason for it."

"Yes," Chuck answered, still struggling with something evasive in his mind.

"Right from the start," Arthur went on, "when Masterson complained about being given a Junior Guide. And then that stunt with the force field, and that brush with the brontosaurs. You've really had your hands full with him, Chuck."

"Why, yes," Chuck said slowly, "I *am* a Junior Guide."

"Why, sure."

"A qualified Junior Guide. And on my eighteenth birthday, after I've completed ten time slips, I'll be a . . . a . . ." He shook his head.

"What's the matter, Chuck?"

"Nothing. I just feel as if I'm discovering all this about myself for the first time. As if I'm . . . I'm being reborn." He grinned ruefully. "That sounds silly, I know."

"How many slips have you been on so far?" Arthur asked.

"Why . . ." Chuck hesitated, concentrating hard. "Five, I think. Yes, this is my fifth." He passed a hand over his forehead. "Funny, I can't seem to think straight. For a minute there, I almost said this was my *first* time slip. I almost said that even though I knew it was my fifth."

"Maybe the earthquake upset you," Arthur offered.

"Yes, maybe," Chuck said, nodding. They kept walking, Chuck's brows still creased in deep concentration. He shook his head again. "I'm sorry, Arthur, but I feel as if I'm forgetting something important. As if a chunk of my mind has been shoved into a dark corner. Do you know what I mean?"

"Slightly."

"It's not a pleasant feeling." He shrugged. "Well, I guess . . ."

"Chuck! Is that you?" The voice was a familiar one.

"Dr. Perry!"

Chuck and Arthur began running toward the sound of the voice. A smile erupted on Chuck's face as he saw the paleontologist step out of the shadows.

"Are you all right, Dr. Perry?"

"Fine, fine." The doctor's voice grew concerned. "Pierre? Dr. Dumar? Is he . . . ?"

"He's fine. We left him with Pete and Denise."

"Well, that's wonderful," Dr. Perry said, his face plainly relieved. "That means the whole party is together again. I've got Masterson and Gardel back there in the ferns."

A wash of disappointment flooded over Chuck. He tried to pinpoint its origin, but he couldn't. "Oh!" he said simply.

"I'll get them," Dr. Perry said.

"Sure." Chuck nodded glumly in the darkness. "Sure."

Denise was sitting up when they reached the geologist and Pete. Her face was pale, and there were tired lines stretching from the wings of her nose down to her bloodless lips, but she managed a weak smile.

Then they found a cave, a simple hole in the face of a sheer jutting cliff, miraculously untouched by the upheaval. They climbed inside like animals seeking shelter from the night. Pete started a fire, mumbling over the loss of their supplies.

"I could use a cup of coffee," Masterson said.

"There ain't any," Pete stated firmly. "There ain't nothing any more. It's all gone."

"I'd *still* like a cup of coffee."

Pete sighed in exasperation. "Maybe you didn't understand me, Mr. Masterson. All our supplies are lost. There ain't . . ."

"I know they're lost," Masterson snapped. "All the more reason why we should head back for the truck."

"*What!*" Arthur asked incredulously.

"I believe I made myself plain and I see no reason why I should repeat myself—to you, of all people."

"But why on earth should we head back for the truck?" Denise asked.

Masterson's face flushed. "It must be obvious to everyone by this time that our young guide has no idea whatever of our present whereabouts."

"That's a lie!" Chuck said.

"Lie or not, we are still nowhere near the rendezvous site. It seems evident that a mistake has been made. I suggest that we head back to where we found Dr. Perry and Dr. Dumar."

"Why?" Chuck wanted to know.

"Because I'm certain the rendezvous site is somewhere near there. Once we reach that spot, we can double back to the truck and get the supplies we'll need for the rest of . . ."

"That's downright ridiculous!" Arthur said. "Why, we're closer to the rendezvous site now than we ever were."

Masterson got to his feet and moved toward Arthur. "See here . . ." he started.

"No," Chuck interrupted. "*You* see here! I'm about

fed up with your half-baked opinions on where we should or shouldn't go. You may have paid for this little jaunt, but you're still a guest of the government, and I'm officially in charge of this expedition."

"Look, Spencer," Masterson said, "when I need advice from a young pup . . ."

"I'm not giving advice," Chuck said, "I'm giving orders. You're in deep enough as it is, Masterson. I haven't forgotten it was you who destroyed the force field. That's a crime, and you'll pay for it when we get back to our own time."

"*If* we get back," Masterson shot.

"We will get back. I've been here before and I know the rendezvous site is near the twin white rocks. In the morning, we'll head for the rocks. With any sort of luck, we should make it."

"I'm not so sure about . . ."

"I think we've had enough discussion," Chuck said, surprised at the sound of his own authority. "I'm tired, and I think the rest of us are, too."

"We'll need an early start," Dr. Perry said softly.

"Then let's turn in," Pete said. "I'm anxious to reach those white rocks."

The morning of the sixth day was a clear one. They stepped out of the cave to be greeted by warm sunlight and glistening greenery. The landscape around them was wet with dew, and the world looked new and shining. It was a wonderful morning.

Except for one thing.

The twin white rocks were gone from the horizon.

Chapter 14 Kidnaped

"THEY'RE gone," Chuck said. He turned frantically to Dr. Perry. "They're gone, sir." His voice fell. "Gone."

Dr. Perry nodded solemnly. "I was afraid of something like this. That upheaval yesterday. It rearranged the topography. Heaven knows where those rocks are now."

Chuck slumped dejectedly. "What now?" he said. His voice caught, and he felt dangerously close to frustrated tears.

Dr. Perry put his arm around Chuck's shoulder. "We'll find a way, Chuck." He grinned amiably. "There's always a way."

Chuck shook his head. "I'm not so sure any more. One thing after another. Almost as if something bigger than we are is trying to keep us here, trying to see that we never get back to our own time."

157

"There's always a way," Dr. Perry repeated. "Remember that, Chuck. You're an awfully young man to be carrying such responsibility, but I'm sure the government's faith in you is not misplaced. We're still alive and healthy and . . ."

"Without food, without a map and with no idea of where the rendezvous site is," Chuck added. "Maybe the government made a mistake."

"I doubt it," Dr. Perry said. "I understand they're pretty careful about whom they choose for important positions."

Chuck didn't answer. He kept staring at the horizon line, wishing that the two rocks would suddenly, magically appear.

"Aren't they?" Dr. Perry persisted. "Isn't there a special course or something?"

"What?"

"Isn't there a special . . ."

"Oh! Yes, yes, there is. Instead of high school. I mean, in addition to high school." Chuck was suddenly confused in his own mind. And yet he had taken the course, hadn't he? Why, yes, certainly. "It's the last two years of high school," he said. "The junior year is spent in studying the period, and the senior year consists of field trips as Junior Guides. The first three time slips are made under the supervision of a Certified Guide. After that, we're on our own. Ten slips are all we need to become Certified Guides ourselves. But you see, Dr. Perry . . ."

"Yes?"

"There's never any trouble. I mean, on my first four slips, all I had to do was put up the force field

and then point out the various animals as they
wandered around it. I don't think the government
even anticipates any trouble. Why should there be
any? If everything goes all right, it's as safe as a
tour of Radio City."

"Of course."

"That's why I'm confused. I feel as if I'm letting
everyone down. I feel like . . . like a kid. A kid
who's lost his way home."

Dr. Perry smiled comfortingly. "You are a kid,
Chuck." He paused and added, "But you'll be a man
when this is all over."

"Sure, if it's *ever* over. I keep thinking we'll be
stuck here forever."

"Somehow, I don't think so."

"Well, what are we going to do? The rocks are
gone."

"What would you suggest?"

Chuck spread his hands helplessly. "I don't know.
I honestly don't know. Before the upheaval, with
the rocks out there . . ." He pointed to the distant
horizon. "I thought it would be simple. Now, with
the rocks gone, I just don't know."

"Where did you say the rocks were?"

Chuck pointed again. "Out there, I guess. But
how can I tell now?"

"But you think they were out that way?"

"Yes, more or less." Chuck shook his head, "Oh,
heck, I just don't know."

"Which way would you lead the party if you had
a choice."

Chuck pointed in the same direction again. "That
way."

"Then suppose we take a chance."

"What!"

"Suppose we follow your instinct and go that way."
Dr. Perry pointed, too.

"But I may be wrong. After all, we can't be sure."

"That's the chance we'll have to take."

"I couldn't ask you to. It may mean the difference
between getting back and staying here forever."

"We'll never get back if we don't try," Dr. Perry
said.

"Yes, but . . ."

"Suppose we put it to a vote."

"Well, I don't know."

"Come on," Dr. Perry said. He took Chuck's arm
and led him back to the party. "Our guide has a
problem," he said. "His markers are gone, and he
has no real way of knowing just where the rendezvous site is any more."

"I figured as much," Masterson said.

"He didn't know from the start," Gardel added.

"Be that as it may," Dr. Perry said, running his
fingers through his thick brown beard, "he thinks
he may know where the rocks *were*."

"Fat chance of that," Gardel put in.

"Has he got a crystal ball?" Masterson asked
sarcastically.

"Oh, pipe down," Pete shouted.

A scowl crossed Masterson's face, and he pressed
his thick lips tightly together. Sitting near him, Dr.
Dumar glanced up through his spectacles, his pale
blue eyes shrewdly analyzing the bigger man.

"Yes," he said at last, "I believe we should allow

my colleague to finish speaking without any further interruptions." He nodded his head in a final motion and then gestured for Dr. Perry to continue.

"The fact is, Chuck feels he shouldn't take the chance without our consent. I suggested that we put it to a vote."

Arthur slammed one big brown fist into the open palm of his other hand. "Good idea. Let's do it and get started."

A smile started at the corners of Dr. Perry's eyes, worked its way down to a flashing grin that gleamed brightly in the depths of his beard. "Unfortunately, we do not seem to be equipped with either pencils or paper. I'm afraid we'll have to make this an open vote."

"Let us proceed," Dr. Dumar said, eying Masterson closely. Masterson tweaked at his nose and then stared at the ground.

"I shall cast my ballot first," Dr. Perry said. "I vote in favor of allowing Chuck to lead us wherever he feels the site may be." Dr. Perry paused. "Now, then. Pierre?"

"Affirmative," Dr. Dumar said.

"Ah, before we go any further," Dr. Perry interrupted, "I think we shall have to abide by a majority vote. Are there any objections to that?" He took the silence for assent and asked, "Arthur?"

"Affirmative," Arthur said. "I'd follow Chuck anywhere."

Chuck smiled at Arthur, feeling a warm inner glow start around his ribs.

"Denise?"

"Affirmative."

"Pete?"

"Affirmative."

"Mr. Masterson?"

"Negative," Masterson said emphatically.

"Gardel?"

"Negative!"

Dr. Perry raised his eyebrows, then ran the palm of his hand over his slightly curving nose. "Ah, do we need a count?"

Dr. Dumar grinned and got to his feet. "I think we should get started," he said. "Chuck, will you lead the way?"

They began moving again.

It was harder now because there were no beacons in the distance to indicate the route. Chuck worked his way through the growth with weary persistence, relying on a sense of direction of which he was none too sure. After awhile he invented a marker on the distant horizon—a slightly rounded hill fuzzy with evergreens. He kept this in sight always, substituting it for the twin white rocks that had once stood out clearly against the sky.

The fuzzy hill became a symbol to him. It stood for home and safety and security.

If he was right.

If he was wrong, it was a meaningless symbol—a hill that was no different from any of the other hills in the Jurassic period. He fervently hoped he was not wrong. The matter went beyond his own personal desires now. He had been given a vote of confidence from the entire group. They had as much as said, "Here, Chuck,

it's yours. We're depending on you to get us out of
this. We have complete faith in you and we'll abide by
any decision you make." He shook his head glumly
as he made his way through the dense undergrowth.
He would have liked to share their confidence in him,
but he couldn't help thinking that he would never
successfully lead them to the rendezvous site. He had
the ominous feeling that they would continue to
wander hopelessly until the land or the beasts finally
claimed the entire party as victims.

The thought was not a cheerful one.

And almost as if nature was doing its best to match
the mood in which Chuck found himself, the day,
which had dawned with a clear blue sky, suddenly
turned gray and dreary. A bone-penetrating dampness
settled over the land, spreading a white mist that
enshrouded the plants.

Chuck led the way. His trousers were soaked to
the waist. The leaves of the plants seemed to acquire
a slippery resiliency when they were wet. They
slapped at him with almost deliberate maliciousness.
They clutched at him with thorny fingers. They tore
at his clothes with spiny claws. They showered cold
water down on him. They grew across the earth in
long hidden trailers that tripped him.

He didn't stop the party.

They kept moving, with Chuck always in the lead,
his eyes on the fuzzy, distant hill that was fast being
swallowed by the spreading mist.

Eventually he forgot where he was.

It was almost as if someone had reached down into
his body and yanked him out. He felt as if he were

standing to one side and stupidly watching a person he knew to be himself go through the motions of fighting the pugnacious terrain. The party stretched behind him like the twisting tail of a kite.

No one complained. Even Masterson was silent as they threaded their slow, torturous way across the face of the earth.

The mist grew thicker, swirling around them like a thin snowstorm now. They grasped hands, struggling forward purposefully. The mist was like a tangible thing, a solid barrier that blinded them and dampened them, penetrating to the marrow, chilling the soul.

At last, even the fuzzy, evergreen-covered hill in the distance was swallowed up.

There was nothing any more. Nothing but an endless cast-iron sky overhead and a shifting, swirling mist that covered them like a soggy blanket. They stumbled over rocks, picking their way over the treacherous ground, fearful lest they tumble into a deep crevice or over the side of a steep rock fault.

Chuck called a halt. He rested one foot on a rock, his arm lying across his knee. Tiredly, he began to speak.

"It's no good," he said. "Everything is against us."

Dr. Perry nodded his head, and his fingers sought the brown beard. He played with the thick hair as he spoke. "What now, Chuck? Where do we go from here?"

Chuck sighed wearily. "I don't know. As long as this fog surrounds us, we can't go on. Unless I can spot the hill again."

"What hill?" Arthur asked.

"Why, the . . ." Chuck passed a hand over his eyes. "I'm sorry. I've been so wrapped up in my own thoughts, I . . ." He stopped and brought the hand over his face, almost as if he were washing some of the weariness away. "I've been using a hill on the horizon as a sort of substitute marker. Now, with this fog, I can't see the hill any more."

Dr. Dumar's voice was gentle when he spoke, his eyes kind behind his spectacles. "What do you plan on doing, Chuck?"

"Well, I want to go ahead by myself."

"What!" Masterson shouted. "You plan on leaving us here."

"Only so that I can find higher ground," Chuck said over Masterson's voice. "If I can, I might be able to see that hill again. It's just a chance."

"I'll go with you," Arthur said.

"No. I'll go alone."

"I'll go with you," Arthur repeated.

"I'd like to come, too," Dr. Perry said.

"But, I . . ."

"What is it, Chuck?"

"I didn't want to endanger anyone's . . . I mean, I thought I should go alone."

"We're coming," Arthur said firmly.

Chuck took quick stock of the situation. Perhaps it would be better if they came along. Three heads should certainly be better than one. "All right," he said quickly. A new thought struck him. If Arthur and Dr. Perry came along, that would leave only Pete, Denise and Dr. Dumar to cope with Masterson and Gardel. Pete was a good man and strong—but Denise was a girl, and Dr. Dumar wasn't exactly a weight lifter.

"I'd like you to come with us too, Gardel," Chuck said suddenly.

Gardel pulled his black brows together into a scowl. "Why?"

"I like your company."

"Don't get smart with me, you little . . ."

Chuck allowed his hand to drop to the .45 at his waist. "I'd like you along, Gardel," he almost whispered.

For an instant it seemed as if Gardel would jump Chuck. Anger flowed between them like live electricity. Then Masterson caught Gardel's eye, and the thin, gaunt man seemed to swallow his anger in one big gulp.

"Sure," he said. "Whatever you say."

"Let's go, then," Arthur said.

Denise walked over to Chuck and looked up into his face. "Chuck, be careful."

"I will," he murmured.

Then they started off.

At the end of an hour Chuck was sorry he'd suggested the trip. They'd climbed every rock they came across, clawing at slippery jagged facings with desperate fingers. In each case the results were the same. The fog was too deep. They couldn't see further than three feet from their noses.

At last Chuck gave up.

"Let's get back," he said. "The rest will be worried."

"Not such a smart stunt, eh, Junior?" Gardel cracked.

"Listen . . ." Chuck started.

"You didn't find your marker and you don't know where the rendezvous site is, either. For a bright boy, you certainly messed things up."

Arthur was beside Gardel instantly. "Shut your mouth," he said.

Gardel turned to face Arthur. His mouth curled back in a sneer. "What?" he asked. "Are you talking to me?"

There was much of Masterson's bluff manner in Gardel, Chuck noticed. He felt uneasy as Arthur moved closer to the man.

"Yes, I'm talking to you, Gardel. You know I'm talking to you."

Gardel looked at the rifle slung on Arthur's back. "Most men talk big when they're carrying guns," he said.

Without hesitation, Arthur unslung the rifle and handed it to Dr. Perry. Gardel grinned a superior grin. "That's much better," he said.

Arthur didn't wait for more. His big, brown fist lashed out in fury, catching Gardel on the side of his jaw. Gardel reeled backward, struggling for balance, and then pulled himself erect. He charged forward, his hands reaching for Arthur's throat.

Arthur hit him twice. A short, solid jab to Gardel's stomach that bent him over double, and then a solid uppercut to the jaw that brought him erect again. Gardel stared at Arthur blankly, and that was when Arthur released the final explosive punch. It caught Gardel on the point of his jaw again. This time he threw his arms back like a bird preparing to fly. He went all the way back, though, hitting the ground with a solid *thwack* that told Chuck just how unconscious he was.

Arthur stood over the man, breathing heavily. "I'm sorry, Chuck. I shouldn't have."

"He deserved it," Chuck answered. He sighed heavily. "I think we'd better get back now."

Arthur reached down and, with one fluid motion, threw Gardel over his shoulder. Together, they started the long trek back to where they'd left the party.

"You've got a nice left," Dr. Perry said.

"Why, thanks," Arthur replied.

Dr. Perry began to chuckle. "As a matter of fact, my friend, your right isn't bad, either. Not bad at all."

Arthur laughed, too, and Chuck found a smile forming on his own face—though he certainly couldn't understand how anything could seem funny in their present predicament.

When they were almost back to where they'd left the party, Gardel regained consciousness. Arthur put him on his feet instantly, and the remainder of the trip was made in silence, with Gardel grumblingly walking a few paces ahead of the other three.

"We should be there soon," Chuck said, at last.

"I don't see anybody," Arthur said.

"This fog," Dr. Perry complained. "We could trip over them before we'd be able to see them."

And that was almost what happened.

They found Pete sprawled over the ground like a crooked stick. He was unconscious, and his rifle was gone.

There was no sign of the rest of the party.

Chapter 15 Pursuit

THEY worked on Pete for a good ten minutes. They
rubbed his wrists and they slapped his face, and
Chuck desperately wished for smelling salts to
revive the portly cook. After awhile his eyelids
blinked, quivered, were still again.

"Pete," Chuck said.

The red-fringed eyelids blinked again and this time
they stayed open to reveal wondering green eyes.

"Wh—where am I?" Pete said classically.

"It's all right, Pete," Chuck murmured.

Pete sat bolt upright, twisting his head to one side.
"Masterson! Where . . . ?"

"He's gone, Pete," Arthur said. "And Dr. Dumar and
Denise with him."

Pete let out a low moan and cradled his head in
his hands.

"What happened?" Dr. Perry wanted to know. Gardel stood by silently, a secret smile on his thin face.

169

"I don't remember exactly," Pete said.

"Try," Dr. Perry prompted.

"Well, it couldn't have happened more than twenty minutes ago. Masterson was all right up to then. After you left, we sat around talking about our chances. Masterson wasn't too happy about the situation, but he wasn't grumbling the way he did. He even said you were a capable guide, Chuck."

"Masterson said that?"

"Yep. His very words."

"You should have smelled a rat right then."

"Well, I thought it was funny at the time, but I figured maybe he was having a change of heart. It looks like I figured wrong."

"What happened?" Dr. Perry asked again.

"Like I said, we were just sitting around. I had the rifle alongside me on the ground while I was talking to Dr. Dumar. He was telling me about France. I learned that Pierre means Pete in French. I got a big kick out of that and I started to laugh. All of a sudden Masterson had the rifle in his hands."

"Ouch!" Arthur said.

"He pointed the gun at me and told me to turn around and put up my hands. When I did that, he ordered Denise and Dr. Dumar to come over to him. Dr. Dumar objected, but Masterson shoved the gun at him and he finally obeyed. I was about to turn around when something hit me on the back of the head." Pete put an exploratory hand to his red hair. "I guess he used the stock of the rifle. Next thing I knew, Chuck was looking down at me, and I was coming up out of a long black tunnel."

"How long ago was this?"

Pete glanced at his watch. "Like I said, it can't be more than twenty minutes."

Chuck got to his feet. "Let's go," he said. "They can't have gone very far in twenty minutes, not with this fog."

Gardel smiled thinly. "I'm staying here," he said.

Chuck turned and there was a cold fury on his face. "Look, Gardel, I've had about enough of you and your rotten boss. If you don't start moving in about three seconds, we'll stake you out and leave you for *Allosaurus*."

"You're bluffing," Gardel said. "You're plain bluffing. I ain't moving from this spot, and you can't force me to."

"No," Chuck said simply. "As a matter of fact, we'll help you stay here. Take him, Arthur."

Arthur moved amazingly fast for a big man. He pinned Gardel's arms behind him, and Chuck said, "Get some stakes, Pete. We'll strip Gardel and use his clothes to tie him to the stakes. *Allosaurus* will appreciate a change of diet, especially when he'll be getting it so easily."

"You're bluffing," Gardel said again, but his voice lacked conviction this time.

"Sure, I'm bluffing."

"We ain't even seen no *Allosaurus* yet," Gardel said. "Maybe there ain't no such animal. Maybe the scientists invented him."

"He's real," Dr. Perry said grimly. "I've seen him many times in the past six months." He shook his head. "He is not a very pleasant beast, Gardel. I don't think you'll get along."

"Maybe they will, Doc," Chuck said. "Gardel isn't a very pleasant beast, either."

Gardel seemed to grow a shade paler. "You . . . you wouldn't really leave me s-s-staked out."

"Of course not," Chuck said. "Ah, here's Pete with some nice chunks of wood now."

Pete dropped a half-dozen sturdy branches at Chuck's feet. "These okay?" he asked.

"Fine. Strip him, Arthur. We've wasted enough time already."

"No," Gardel shouted. "I'll come along. I'll . . . I'll come along."

Chuck shoved him ahead of the group. "Remember this, Gardel, and remember it well. I wasn't kidding. I'd be a fool to waste time arguing with you. I was going to leave you staked here as sure as you're living. Just remember that."

Gardel didn't answer.

Chuck felt Arthur's hand on his shoulder.

"Easy," Arthur said. "Don't lose your grip."

"I'm all right," Chuck said. "Let's get moving."

They found tracks. Three sets of footprints. The smallest set belonged to Denise, the next largest to Dr. Dumar. The heavy footprints that dug down deep into the earth were Masterson's.

They followed the tracks diligently like big-game hunters close to their quarry. At one point they found a spot where the group must have paused to rest. Chuck examined the spot closely. Masterson's cigar had sprinkled ash all over the ground, and his footprints were deeper, as if he'd stood in one spot for a long time.

"Let's go," Chuck said.

The tracks were clear, disappearing only when the fugitives crossed a large expanse of rock, but picking up again whenever they hit soft earth. The fog was beginning to lift a little, and the going was easier and faster. Chuck was thankful for that. Masterson had had to contend with the fog and with two prisoners who had gone along with him unwillingly. Now that the fog was lifting, Chuck had every hope of catching up. And then . . ?

He didn't know. He didn't know what would happen because he couldn't figure what possible motive had provoked Masterson. He could only conclude that the man was completely insane. Why else would he pull a fool stunt like this? What could he possibly hope to gain?

And why had he taken only Denise and Dr. Dumar with him? Why leave Pete behind? Chuck felt certain there was meaning to that. It would have been more difficult to have taken Pete along, of course. He would have presented a constant menace to Masterson. Whatever his reasons for escape had been, he would not want them menaced. On the other hand, had he taken Pete with him, the returning hill hunters might have concluded that they were simply lost, had somehow missed Masterson, Pete, Denise and Dr. Dumar in the deep fog.

That would have seemed to be the best plan. And yet Masterson had left Pete behind.

He had done that for a good reason, Chuck surmised. It was obvious why he wanted his niece with him. Apparently he was a human being, after all, and was concerned over her welfare.

But why Dr. Dumar?

Chuck felt this was the key. If he knew why Masterson had taken the geologist with him, he'd also know why Masterson had pulled his escape at all.

"Gardel," he called, "wait up."

Gardel stopped in his tracks and waited for Chuck to join him. He pulled his lips back over his teeth and said, "What is it, Superboy?"

"Don't get smart, Gardel," Chuck warned.

"Tough guy," Gardel snarled. "A real tough guy."

"Sure," Chuck said sarcastically. "I chew spikes and spit out carpet tacks."

"A comedian, too."

"Why did your boss leave the party?" Chuck asked suddenly.

"Because he . . ." Gardel snapped his jaws shut and allowed a smile to trickle across his thin mouth. "How do I know why he left?" he amended. "You think I'm a mind reader?"

"He must want to hunt dinosaurs pretty badly," Chuck said.

"Yeah, that's it. He wants to hunt a little."

"Then why does he need Dr. Dumar with him?" Chuck snapped.

"Maybe the little man is a good hunter, too. Or maybe Dirk wanted a guide. Maybe he . . ."

"A guide," Chuck said slowly.

Gardel turned and glanced at him, pivoting his head back quickly. "Or maybe he took the doc along as protection. Who knows?" He smiled his thin smile and added, "He's got him, though, and that's tough."

"It's tough, all right," Chuck agreed. "The authorities will think it's very tough. And Masterson may find prison a little different from what he imagined."

Gardel laughed out loud, his thin nose jutting up into the air, his lips pulling back over large teeth. "You got to get him first," he said.

"We'll do that, Gardel. We'll do that."

They lost the trail shortly after that.

The footprints ended when a large bed of slate claimed the land. The slate stretched for as far as the eye could see, covering the ground with gray monotony. It was spread about in a crude semicircle, and Masterson could have turned anywhere on the bed to plunge into the undergrowth. It would take them at least a half-hour to walk the perimeter of the semicircle. By that time Masterson could be a good distance away.

"This isn't so good," Dr. Perry said.

Pete nodded his red head. "That's putting it mildly, Doc."

Gardel said nothing. He simply smiled.

"Let's split up," Chuck said. "Pete, Dr. Perry, cut clear across the bed to the other side. Then start back, walking the perimeter and looking for sign on the edges. Arthur and I will start on this end and we'll work toward the middle, too. Whoever spots tracks first will call the others." He paused and looked intently at Gardel. "You can come with Arthur and me, Gardel."

"Sure," Gardel said. "Why not?"

Chuck watched Pete and Dr. Perry start across the slate, heading for the other end of the semicircle.

"This isn't going to be easy," Chuck said to Arthur.

"It may be easier than you think."

"How so?"

"I've been on a lot of hunting expeditions in the

ten years I worked for Masterson. I can track like an Indian scout."

"I'm glad to hear that," Chuck said, as they started around the semicircle, shoving aside the plants on the perimeter so that they could study the ground for tracks.

"That was the one thing I really enjoyed," Arthur said. "The hunting. Even before I started working for Masterson, I used to hunt in the woods back home. I was pretty good."

"Really?"

Arthur nodded, thinking back to the past. "As a matter of fact, I was offered a job with an expedition that was heading for Africa just about the time Masterson came along. The job with Masterson sounded better, so I took it." He shook his head. "Brother, did I make a mistake."

"Well, you had no way of knowing."

They were still threading their way around the slate bed, painstakingly studying every inch of the ground.

"Sure," Arthur said, "but I often wonder what would have become of me if Masterson hadn't come along at just that time. The man about to hire me was a wonderful old guy. As a matter of fact, when he died, he left a great deal of money to one of the boys he'd hired for that expedition. I remember reading about it in the newspapers at the time. A grand old guy."

"What was his name?" Chuck asked.

"J. D. Daniels. Have you ever heard of him?"

Chuck stopped short in his tracks. "Why he was a multimillionaire, Arthur. Brother, I'll say you made a mistake."

Arthur agreed, nodding his head. "Well, there was no way of knowing at the time. Sometimes, though, I wish that Masterson had never existed, that I'd never met him."

"You'd still be in the gutter if it hadn't been for Dirk," Gardel cracked, a malicious grin on his face.

"Gardel," Chuck warned, "didn't you learn a lesson the last time you shot your mouth off at Arthur?"

"He doesn't bother me." Arthur said. "I feel sorry for him, that's all."

In spite of what he had said, though, Arthur fell into a deep, brooding silence that made Chuck want to punch Gardel's gloating face. They continued around the slate arc, and Chuck began to wonder if Masterson hadn't simply leaped into the air and disappeared that way.

And then Arthur yelled, "Hey!"

"What is it?"

"A cigar," he said. He got down on his hands and knees and shoved some ferns aside. Gingerly, he picked up a smoldering brown cigar stub. "It's still warm, Chuck. He couldn't have dropped it long ago."

"Maybe he dropped it on purpose. He may be trying to throw us off."

"Maybe," Arthur said. He shoved some more ferns aside, practically putting his nose to the ground. "No! No, Chuck, here's a footprint! They went this way."

Chuck didn't wait for more. He cupped his hands to his mouth and shouted, "Pete! Dr. Perry! We've picked up the trail again!"

From far off at the other end of the semicircle, he heard Pete shout, "Leave a marker, Chuck! Get going!"

The voice echoed over the land, coming up out of the dispersing mist like the voice of a ghost. Chuck quickly removed his shirt and dropped it to the slate.

"I'm leaving my shirt," he yelled. "My shirt, Pete!"

"Right-o," the shout came back. "We'll find it. Get going."

"Let's go," Chuck said to Arthur.

They moved off the slate into the thick growth. Chuck stumbled forward eagerly, anxious to catch up with Masterson and his prisoners. He ignored the plants that tore at his exposed chest. His excitement mounted as the footprints grew clearer. The growth was thinning now, the land becoming strewn with loose rocks. The mist still clung to their waists, but it had cleared considerably, and he could see a sheer, high cliff in the distance, sitting across their line of approach like a gigantic flat tombstone. As they got closer to the cliff, Chuck saw that it was broken by a ledge some fifty feet from the ground, giving the appearance of a crude step cut into its face. The bottom of the cliff was strewn with huge boulders that formed a labyrinthine wall where the cliff met the land.

"What do you think?" Arthur asked.

"I don't know," Chuck said. "He may have skirted the boulders and the cliff."

"Maybe. The ground looks pretty rugged, though."

"Yeah. What do you think?"

"I think he's holed up among those boulders at the bottom of the cliff."

"Let's hope not."

"Be a heck of a job to get him out if he is. Especially with him holding Denise and Dr. Dumar."

Chuck glanced over his shoulder, hoping that Pete and Dr. Perry had spotted his shirt. "We'll have help soon," he said. "That should make the job easier."

"Ever try to get a gopher out of its hole?" Arthur asked.

"No."

"It's a tough job. An almost impossible job."

"Well," Chuck said, "Masterson isn't a gopher."

Arthur chuckled softly. "More a rat, I would say."

Chuck smiled with him, then laid a hand on his powerful arm. "Let's get a little closer. Keep low."

They dropped down low to their knees, walking in a half-crouch. They hadn't traveled three feet when a booming voice shouted, "Don't move another inch or I'll shoot the girl!"

Chapter 16 Counterplot

As IF backing up the voice, a rifle sounded from behind the boulders. The bullet whistled through the air, kicking up a spurt of rock and dust some six inches from Chuck's nose. He swallowed hard and began rolling toward a low flat rock to his left. The rifle boomed again, and Chuck heard the same whistle, was relieved when he saw the bullet plow up dirt far short of its mark. A high shrill laugh came from behind the boulders, and Chuck shuddered when he heard it. Arthur was beside him now, flat on his belly behind the rock. Gardel was there, too, smiling in superiority.

"Kind of got you, ain't he, Superboy?"

"Shut up, Gardel."

Gardel laughed. "Give it to 'em, Dirk," he shouted.

Masterson's voice came back over the space between them and the boulders. "That you, Brock?"

"Give them another round," Gardel called.

"Come on over," Masterson shouted.

The .45 was in Chuck's hand almost before Gardel moved an inch.

"If you want a hole in your head, go on," Chuck said. "Otherwise, get down on your belly and stretch out your hands in front of you." He wiggled the .45 at Gardel, and the thin man eyed it with curious respect. This was a language he understood. Guns. And violence. These were the elements that had gone into the shaping of his character.

"He's got me," Gardel called. "The kid is armed."

When Masterson's voice came back, it was cold and deadly. "Chuck! Chuck Spencer! Can you hear me?"

"I hear you, Masterson."

"Get this right the first time, because I'm not going to repeat it. Who's with you?"

"None of your business!"

"Who's with you?" Masterson shouted again.

Chuck was about to answer when he heard Pete's voice behind him. "Chuck, where are you?"

"Get down, Pete!" he shouted. "Masterson's holed up here and he's using the rifle."

"Right," Pete's voice came.

Chuck kept the .45 trained at the boulders. Arthur had already unslung his rifle and had it resting on the rock. He aimed along the barrel at the boulders and waited for Masterson to show some sign of himself. Behind them, they heard scraping sounds as Pete and Dr. Perry worked their way toward the protection of the rock. Masterson shouted, "I see you!" and triggered off a shot that nearly planted itself in Pete's leg. Pete pulled the leg in, breathed a deep sigh and continued to crawl toward the rock, Dr. Perry behind him. Arthur opened fire, peppering the boulders with a steady stream of bullets that discouraged Masterson from taking any more pot shots at the approaching duo.

When they reached the rock, Chuck quickly explained the situation to them. Arthur had stopped firing, but he kept watching the boulders.

"Looks like a stalemate to me," Dr. Perry said.

"Yes," Chuck agreed, "unless we can talk some sense into him."

"Chuck Spencer!" Masterson's voice boomed again. It bounced off the boulders, echoed in a thousand darkened shadows, echoed in the very pockmarks of time itself.

"I'm here, Masterson."

"Send Gardel over. Send him right now."

"He's not going anywhere," Chuck yelled back.

Gardel tried to rise, but Arthur slammed one meaty hand into the small of his back, and he bounced back against the ground again, the wind knocked out of him.

"Send him over or I'll shoot Denise," Masterson said.

Dr. Perry's eyes widened. "Why, the man is insane!"

"He's bluffing," Pete said. "He wouldn't shoot his own niece."

"Try him and see," Gardel muttered.

"Gardel stays with us," Chuck shouted back.

"I'm not kidding," Masterson said. "I'm not fooling, Spencer. I'll shoot her if you don't send Gardel over."

Chuck heard Denise shout, "Don't believe . . ." Her voice was cut off, as if a hand had been clamped over her mouth.

"You're bluffing," Chuck shouted. "And we're calling your bluff."

Dr. Perry's eyes took on an anxious look. "Chuck, are you sure you're . . ."

There was a deadly silence now. It seemed to hang over the land like a mailed fist. The fog was almost all gone, but the sky was still a leaden gray. Chuck saw a small reptile scamper across the no man's land between the rock and the boulders. *The Jurassic*, he thought. *Jurassic. Jurassic. Jurassic.*

The silence continued, and Chuck waited with his heart in his mouth.

"Send him over," Dr. Perry said. "Send Gardel over or he'll shoot the girl."

"What's to stop him from shooting her once he gets Gardel?" Chuck asked.

"The man is a maniac, can't you see? Why should we provoke him?"

"I think you're wrong, Doc," Chuck said. "He's more than a maniac. He's got something up his sleeve. If we send Gardel over, we'll be playing right into his hands."

"You gamble real pretty with somebody else's life," Gardel muttered. "Maybe Denise don't feel the way you do about it."

There was silence again. Chuck waited, his ears straining for the sound of a bolt being shoved home.

Finally Masterson said, "All right, Spencer, I'll make a bargain with you. I'll send Denise back safely."

"All right," Chuck said. "Send her over."

"I said a bargain, not a gift. I'll trade Denise for Gardel and Dr. Perry."

"What?"

"You heard me. Send over Gardel and Dr. Perry, and the girl is yours."

"Tell him we'll do it," Dr. Perry said quickly.

"No!" Chuck snapped. Something was beginning to take shape in his mind. He began to wonder all over again about Masterson's reasons for taking Dr. Dumar with him and leaving Pete behind. Dr. Dumar was undoubtedly valuable to him, whereas Pete was not. Now he wanted Dr. Perry. Why?

He remembered the mining equipment he had seen in the truck that day he had unloaded supplies. Suddenly it became perfectly clear to him.

Uranium!

Of course! Why the entire time slip had probably been an excuse for Masterson to get back here where he could get his hands on the uranium deposit. He'd probably read all about it in the newspapers and decided to come back to the Jurassic to find the scientists and the deposit. That explained the mining equipment in the truck and it explained Masterson's motive for smashing the force field. A hunter, indeed! He was hunting, all right. He was hunting for a fortune in uranium, and the only men who could lead him to it were Dr. Dumar and Dr. Perry.

Now Chuck understood why Masterson had constantly wanted to return to the spot where the two doctors had been found. He had probably assumed that the deposit was somewhere in that vicinity and had tried to lead the party that way, rather than back to the rendezvous site. He'd probably known all along that Chuck was heading in the right direction—but a return to his own time was the farthest thing from his mind. At least, until he'd got all the uranium he needed.

This gave Chuck another interesting thought. How had Masterson planned on getting away with it? He'd find the deposit, yes, probably by getting "lost" from the party and searching for the two scientists until he found them. Then what? If he left the doctors alive, his plans would be ruined. Had he then planned on killing them?

"What do you say, Spencer?" Masterson shouted. "Denise for Gardel and Dr. Perry."

Chuck snapped his thoughts back to the immediate problem. "Dr. Perry," he said anxiously, "who has the map to the uranium deposit?"

"Why . . . why . . ."

"I know it's top secret stuff, but this is important. Does Dr. Dumar have it?"

"No."

"Then you do."

"No."

Chuck's eyes opened wide in disbelief. "Well . . . well, who does?"

"The Jurassic has it, Chuck."

"I don't understand."

"Pierre had it in his sleeping bag with him on the night of the upheaval. In all the excitement . . ."

"He left it in the bag!"

"It's not as bad as it sounds. We still remember the location. We spent a lot of time there, Chuck. We could probably draw it from memory—if the upheaval didn't change the situation."

"What do you say, Spencer?" Masterson shouted.

"I say NO!" Chuck roared. "I don't like your bargain, Masterson. It smells."

Hastily, Chuck lowered his voice and told Dr. Perry, Pete and Arthur what he thought. He watched their faces as he spoke, saw Dr. Perry nod.

"I was wondering why he was so friendly to us when we first joined the party," Dr. Perry said. "I should have realized he was after something."

"We've got to stall him," Chuck said. "We've got to get that rifle away from him. If he gets you over there with Dr. Dumar, he'll force the location of the deposit out of you. And when he's through with you . . ."

"Mmm," Dr. Perry agreed.

Chuck's eyes wandered over to the cliff, climbed the sheer wall to settle on the ledge fifty feet from the ground.

"That's it," he said aloud.

"What? What's what?" Arthur asked.

"The ledge." Chuck indicated it with a motion of his head, not wanting Masterson to see him pointing. "If I can get up to that ledge without Masterson seeing me, we'll have him boxed in."

"How the deuce you going to get up there?" Pete asked.

"I don't know. Around the side, maybe. The sides don't look as steep as the face. I'd have to go up the side anyway, or Masterson would see me."

"You'll never do it," Arthur said. "It's too steep a climb."

"I've got to try."

"Why not me?" Arthur asked.

"Because I'm the alleged guide on this time slip,"

Chuck said quietly. "So far, all I've done is get us into a lot of trouble. Maybe I can get us out of some now."

Arthur's eyes met Dr. Perry's, and the paleontologist nodded imperceptibly. Chuck saw the movement and smiled. "I'm not trying to be a hero or a martyr, believe me. I just feel ... I feel as if I've ... as if I haven't been doing my job. Do you know what I mean? As if I've let everyone down."

Dr. Perry was quiet for a long time. Then he said, "Every man has his mountain to climb, Chuck. Do a good job with it."

"Thanks," Chuck said. "Now here's my plan. . . ."

The ground was rough, covered with sharp rocks that stabbed at his hands and his chest and his knees. He kept close to the ground, hugging it for dear life as he moved away from the protection of the rocks. Behind him, he heard the sharp crack of a rifle as Arthur began his diversionary fire. He did not turn to look back. He kept his head low and his body pressed flat to the terrain as he inched his way toward the boulders and the sheer face of the cliff. The rifle fire stopped suddenly, and then the second part of his plan went into action.

"Masterson!"

"Yeah, what is it?"

"This is Dr. Perry talking."

"What's on your mind, Dr. Perry?"

"I've been talking to the boy. Spencer. I've been talking to him."

"Is that what all the shooting was about, Dr. Perry?"

"The shooting was the boy's idea. I've talked him out of it. He thinks the way I do now."

"And just how do you think?"

"I've decided to accept your proposition. Gardel and I will join you if you give us Denise in return."

He moved forward more quickly now. The land still probed at him with a hundred razor-sharp fingers, but he was out of Masterson's line of vision and he could proceed without caution. Slowly he got to his feet and began running in a wide arc, circling around the boulders, heading for the side of the cliff. He smiled as he heard Dr. Perry speaking. Filibuster. Good old American filibuster. A filibuster in the Age of Reptiles. The thought amused him, but he was not forgetting the task that lay ahead of him.

"I'll send Gardel over first."

"I'm listening."

"When Gardel gets there, Masterson, you'll send Denise to us. Then I'll come over to you."

"That's rather shrewd, Dr. Perry, but I don't like it."

"Why not?"

"What's to prevent you from getting Denise and then not coming over to me yourself?"

"The thought hadn't even entered my mind."

"I'll bet it hadn't, Dr. Perry. Do you take me for a fool?"

"I give you my word of honor. As soon as Denise is safely here, I shall start across to you."

"I'm sorry. I don't like the arrangement."

"Don't you trust me, Masterson?"

"I do not trust *anyone*, Doctor."

"Well, what's your suggestion, then?"

The ground swelled upward to become a ring of boulders that ran around the side of the cliff. Chuck studied the boulders for a moment, pausing to catch his breath. And then he started to climb. Mounting the boulders was not too difficult, and he accomplished it with ease. Now only the cliff lay above him. Fifty feet up its side was a narrow ledge from which he could get a clear shot at Masterson if the situation was pressed that far. He hoped it wouldn't be. The .45 was heavy on his waist as he reached for his first foothold on the sloping side of the cliff.

"Hello, Masterson?"

"I'm still here."

"Do you have any suggestions?"

"I'm thinking."

"Suppose you send Denise over first? Then when she's here, Gardel and I can come over together."

"Do you take me for an idiot?"

"Why? The idea sounds reasonable, Masterson."

"To you, perhaps. But you're four men there, and Gardel is only one. How do I know you won't jump him as soon as the girl is in your camp?"

"We wouldn't do that, Masterson."

"How do I *know* you won't?"

"You'll just have to take my word for it."

"In fact, Doctor, how do I know that Gardel isn't bound and gagged right this minute? How do I know this isn't just a trick to get the girl back to you?"

"That would be foolish, Masterson. You'd still have Dr. Dumar with you. You'd still have one hostage."

"Let me see Gardel. Have him step out from behind the rock!"

He was almost to the ledge. His heart gave a vicious leap when he heard Masterson's last request. He hadn't counted on that. He hadn't even considered it when forming his plan. He kept climbing, reaching for shrubs that jutted from the rocky side, tearing at the slope with grasping fingers. Ten feet. Ten more feet. Seven feet. He could see the rock far below him, with Arthur and Pete sprawled behind it. Dr. Perry yanked Gardel to his feet and pulled the gaunt man with him out into the open. Arthur's rifle swung around slowly, pointed at the back of Gardel's head. Five more feet.

"Here he is, Masterson."

"Hello, Brock!"

"H-h-hello, Dirk."

"What do you think, Brock? Shall I trust them? How does their plan sound to you?"

"I . . . I don't know, Dirk."

"You sound kind of nervous. What's the matter? Is anything wrong, Brock?"

Another foot. One more foot. His hands reached out for the flatness of the ledge. He got a good grip on the surface and then slowly swung his legs onto it. He could see Masterson behind the protection of his boulder now, far below. The big man had a rifle, and it was pointed across the clearing at Dr. Perry and

Gardel. Slowly, cautiously, he unholstered the .45 at his waist, checked the clip and released the safety. He looked down again, saw Denise and Dr. Dumar huddled on Masterson's right. From the other side of the cliff, beyond his own vision and beyond Masterson's, he heard a curious sound. A scraping sound or the sound of something treading on loose rocks. He was just turning his head to locate the source of the sound when Gardel pulled his arm away from Dr. Perry. He started to run across the clearing, and his mouth was open in a hoarse warning.

"Look out, Dirk! The boy! With a gun!"

Chapter 17 King of the Beasts

I T ALL happened very suddenly and yet it seemed to take ages. From his perch on the ledge, Chuck viewed the entire scene stretched out below him. He had the vague impression that he was sitting in the balcony and watching a play on an immense stage. Gardel's shout served as a signal, and everything followed from it—like the opening gun in a horse race or the bell in a prize fight. Gardel shouted and ripped away from Dr. Perry, starting across the clearing toward the boulders.

But Gardel hadn't pointed and he hadn't looked up. He'd done nothing to indicate where Chuck was, and Masterson had no way of knowing.

Masterson reacted the way any man in his position would have. The situation had been a tense one up to then, and his finger was probably curled nervously around the trigger of his rifle. When Gardel shouted, he pulled the trigger all the way.

He didn't aim. He fired blindly across the clearing and he continued to fire.

Gardel screamed and threw his head back, clutching at the steel-jacketed slugs that were ripping into his chest.

"Brock!" Masterson shouted. He stopped shooting. The ragged edges of his voice seeped into the land. The smoke from his rifle rose in a mournful black cloud that hung over his head like a specter of doom and then vanished.

"Brock!" he called again.

Gardel dropped to his knees, his fingers threaded with the red strands of blood that spilled from his torn chest.

He staggered forward, moving on his knees, leaving a trail of blood behind him.

"Dirk—Dirk—" His voice was a dry whisper, the voice of a man a hundred million years from all other men, the dry voice of a man who was dying in a strange time, in a strange land. There was fright in the voice and a pathetic disbelief. He could not understand why Masterson had shot him, and worse, he could not understand why he should be dying at this time.

He pitched forward on his face, rolled over onto his back and spread his arms.

Brock Gardel would do no more wondering.

"Brock! I didn't . . . *Brock!*" The last was almost a scream. Masterson was alone now. It was Masterson against the land and Masterson against his fellow men, and Masterson against whatever conscience he had. Chuck dropped to his belly and shouted, "All right, Masterson, it's all over now."

Masterson whirled, bringing up the rifle and triggering off a fast shot.

Chuck hugged the ledge, his face and chest pressed against the coarse rock. He heard the strange sound again, far off to Masterson's left. The sound of . . . of hoofs. Above that sound, the terrible soul-shattering cry of a nonhuman thing.

Masterson heard the sound, too, and he turned rapidly, bringing the gun to bear on the boulders over to his left.

It appeared suddenly.

There was nothing at first. Only boulders and a gray sky and an alien land.

And then the land was filled. The thing blotted out the sky, reared high on its hind legs. The blood cry tore from its throat again, and Chuck froze to the ledge, unable to move, his muscles paralyzed.

Allosaurus!

At last, like the star of the show putting in a late appearance. This was the fierce carnivore; this was one of the master beasts. Tall as a monarch he stood, thirteen feet high, thirty-four feet from the gaping, open jaws to the end of his tail.

He bellowed to the sky and bellowed to the land, bellowed his superiority to the puny man who crouched behind the boulders with a rifle in his hands.

Allosaurus was green, a dull green, the green of a tarnished penny. His eyes were cold and flat, and his open jaws revealed teeth a full three inches long. The jaws snapped shut, and the teeth gnashed furiously. And then the jaws were open again, revealing the fearsome, razor-sharp teeth, exposing a yawning red maw in the twenty-seven-inch-long head. He held his short forefeet close to his massive chest. He took a long, hunched stride forward, the powerful muscles of his hind limbs shoving him over the ground.

"No! No!" Masterson screamed.

The claws on the beast's hind legs scraped on the rocky ground as he came forward hungrily. His flat eyes gleamed malevolently. Saliva dripped from his jaws, and a deep rumbling came from within his enormous body. Those claws and jaws could tear and rip. They could penetrate the armor-like hides of his contemporaries, slashing them to bits, cleaning their carcasses to the bone. This was no minor beast. This was one of the kings, one of the fiercest, flesh-eating land animals ever known to Man.

He dwarfed Masterson. He came closer to the boulders. His scream chilled the blood, quickened the heart. It was impossible not to know fear. There was something about the monster that brought fear immediately. Not his size alone, and not the knowledge that he was extremely dangerous. It was something else. A fear that sprang up full-grown. A fear that made Chuck want to run, but that made him incapable of running. A fear that froze muscles, mind, heart, body. A fear that chilled him, yet covered him with sweat. A fear that was a living thing inside. Fear! Real fear. Fear that crackled along Chuck's skin like a blazing thunderbolt. Fear that crawled in his belly and turned his knees to mud. Fear such as Chuck had never experienced before.

Chuck knew that fear and he knew that Masterson was experiencing it, too. The horrible cry ripped at the sky again, provoking insanity, gripping the skin in a shivering, clammy grasp.

"No!" Masterson shouted again. Suddenly he was firing the rifle. The beast opened its jaws wide, the loose skin around its throat tightening with the motion. Masterson fired until the gun was empty and then he loaded it with trembling fingers. Dr. Dumar and Denise were far to Masterson's right. Chuck saw them edging their way toward the clearing, ready to make a break for it.

Masterson's bullets seemed to do no good at all. If anything, they simply infuriated the beast more. Chuck knew, then, that Masterson was firing at the dinosaur's tough hide, where he could hope to do no damage. A bullet between the eyes might stop the beast—but his eyes were in his head, and his head towered far above Masterson.

It did not tower above Chuck.

From his position on the ledge, he could get a clear shot at *Allosaurus*.

He caught his breath, feeling a hot lump in his throat. What if his fire drew the beast to him? *Allosaurus* was closer now, much closer. The jaws snapped at Masterson now. In a little while it would be all over.

Slowly, fear making his hand tremble, Chuck raised the .45.

"Owen."

He took aim, looking down the length of his shaking arm.

"Owen."

The voice whispered across his memory, gently, gently, like a mild breeze soughing over a cold mountaintop. "Owen," it called. "Owen."

His finger hesitated on the trigger. His brow curled, and his memory struggled with the name, pondered it, frantically wrestled with it until he was almost on the verge of tears. He looked at Masterson, and the name whispered across his mind again. He did not pull the trigger.

Then the voice was gone, his mind was clear and the name was forgotten. There was left only a great awareness of the sharp outline of figures against a background of gray sky. *Allosaurus* lunged, and the automatic leaped in Chuck's hand at the same time. He fired again, saw the blossoms of red sprout between the beast's eyes, saw its jaws snap on Masterson's body at the same time.

Masterson screamed, a terrifying scream that curled Chuck's stomach into a rigid ball. He kept squeezing the trigger until he'd fired the seven shells in the clip. He unslung the rifle then and kept blasting away at the bloody, gigantic head. The jaws stopped working, opened wide to reveal teeth crimson with Masterson's blood. Masterson dropped to the ground like a stone, and *Allosaurus* wobbled backward. His hind legs gripped unsteadily at the ground, his forefeet drooping weakly. Suddenly the beast toppled over like a giant tree falling. Down, down, he came, hitting the ground with a shock that caused the surrounding rocks to tremble. A great cloud of dust rose over the beast, covered him like a shroud and settled over his thick hide. He lay there in a spreading pool of his own blood, motionless, the flat eyes blank.

Allosaurus was dead.

Chuck looked down the face of the cliff to where Masterson lay crumpled against the rocks. One look told him all he had to know.

Masterson was dead, too.

Chapter 18 Home Again

CHUCK stood on the ledge for a long time. He looked down at Denise, cradled in Dr. Dumar's arms, sobbing gently. He glanced again at Masterson, a broken man with broken dreams. His eyes wandered to *Allosaurus,* the blood still gushing from his enormous head. The scavenger reptiles were already scrambling over the rocks, heading for the dead hulk, ready to tear it to pieces.

He looked toward the horizon, far out over the land. The sky was clear. The sun slanted down in fanlike rays, bathing the land in a golden wash of warmth. His eyes roamed past the boulders, past the rock-strewn clearing, past the bordering fringe of shrubbery, past the deeper greenery beyond that.

He opened his eyes wider.

His mouth came unhinged and his features fought the grin that tried desperately to form on his face. A shout rose in his throat, strangled itself. He wanted to laugh wildly and cry hysterically, and all he could do was stand there and shiver like an autumn leaf on a shedding tree.

Far off in the distance, looking like the outline of a postage stamp on the ground, was the white square that had been painted to mark off the exact relay area!

"Hey!" he shouted. "Hey! We've found it!"

He pointed wildly, looking down at Arthur, Dr. Perry and Pete as they ran across the clearing.

"What?" Arthur yelled. "What, Chuck?"

"The rendezvous site! Over that way! We'll get home, after all!"

His wrist watch said one o'clock.

They had traveled until dusk and then stopped for the night, because they did not want to lose their way by wandering hopelessly in the darkness. On the morning of the seventh day they had started their trek again—and now it was one o'clock.

Chuck glanced at his watch briefly. One o'clock. If they did not reach the relay area by two o'clock . . .

Doggedly, he led the party forward.

He tried not to think of the time limit imposed on the party. Instead, he tried to formulate the nature of the report he would make to the authorities. Somehow, though, the report did not seem very important. Someone named Masterson had paid for the expedition. But Masterson was dead.

He found it difficult to remember much about the man, although he knew that he should, because he did, after all, have to make a report. Somewhat vaguely, his mind struggled with the concept of Masterson's and Gardel's deaths. He knew he had thought over this very same problem not too long ago—but he didn't know why. He understood clearly that Masterson and Gardel had ceased to exist long before they had been born—and he knew that the time stream would therefore make adjustments to account for their nonexistence. He knew, too, that eventually he would completely forget that either of the two men had existed. He knew this with a dead certainty. Yet he did not know *why* he knew it. He accepted it calmly as a fact. His store of experience told him that he had encountered this very same situation—or a parallel one—sometime not too long ago. He could not remember what that situation had been. He knew, though, that the memory of Masterson would fade, that he and his gaunt assistant would slowly slide into oblivion, leaving a completely adjusted set of circumstances, a set of circumstances that discounted the existence of the two men, that substituted a completely new train of events.

The idea was a strange one, but a familiar one. That he could not account for its familiarity did not disturb him.

He did wonder, however, how the time stream would adjust to Masterson's absence. It would have to go all the way back, back to the beginnings, back to long before Chuck had even met the man. All traces of Masterson and Gardel would be erased, all contacts with any other men, all influences he may have had on the shaping of their characters or lives.

It was an elementary law. A thing cannot *be* and *not be* at the same time. Masterson had either existed or he had not existed. If he had died in the Jurassic, he could not have existed in modern times. And if he had not existed in modern times, then someone else had financed the expedition, someone else had hired Chuck.

Chuck did not know who that someone else could be.

Pete drew up alongside him and shook his head. "Chuck, I got a problem."

Chuck glanced at his watch again. 1:10. Time was running out. Sifting through his hands like so many tiny particles of sand. At 2:00 P.M. the mechanism of the Time Slip would whir into operation. If they were within the white square, they would be jolted back to their own time. If they were not, the Slip would bring back nothing.

"What is it, Pete?" he asked.

"I keep feeling that somebody is missing from the party. That's screwy, I know, because we're all here. But something keeps tickling my mind. It says, 'Master gone,' or something like that. You know what I mean? I keep trying to remember clearly, but I can't. It's like something is slipping out of my mind and I can't stop it."

"I know what you mean, Pete."

It was already happening. Masterson was sliding out of Pete's memory, soon to be forgotten completely. And even as Chuck thought of the dead man, he found it difficult to remember what he'd worn, what he'd smoked—pipe, cigarette, cigar? What kind of voice did he have? He vaguely sensed that the man had caused a great deal of trouble, but all he could remember was the incident with *Allosaurus*. Even that was only an indistinct impression. Masterson in the beast's jaws, Chuck firing wildly, blood spurting, death.

"I guess it's nothing to worry about," Pete said half-heartedly. "But still, it's a funny feeling. Like I'm maybe losing my marbles."

"You're perfectly sane, Pete," Chuck said. "I'd forget all about it if I were you."

Pete laughed a little. "Looks like I'm going to forget all about it whether I want to or not. The darnedest part is that I can't remember what I'm supposed to be forgetting!"

1:15.

1:20.

Time was a living thing. It slithered across the face of Chuck's watch like a Jurassic reptile. It was just as deadly. It had no regard for Chuck or anyone in the group. It moved swiftly, blindly, oblivious to the torturous pace the party was keeping. It was not easy, this pace. It had never been easy. With time hovering over their heads like a deadly guillotine, it was more difficult.

They did not stop to rest.

They kept moving, the breath raging in their lungs. Their clothes were soaked with perspiration. Their faces were gaunt, their eyes sunken, flickering with doubt.

Chuck spoke to each of them briefly. He did not offer encouragement, did not bother with pep talks. He simply prodded them, kept them moving when they would have stopped, needled them the way a man would shove his cattle along a dusty road. In his brief talks he learned that Masterson had all but faded from their minds. He still did not know how the time stream had adjusted to Masterson's nonexistence. If Master-

son had not financed the expedition, someone had.
Someone with a great deal of money. Who?

He didn't know, and in a little while Masterson
became a faint blur in his memory.

By 1:30 he could not remember Masterson at all.
1:30.

There was not much time now. There was not much
time at all. He began to worry in earnest. The worry
hung around him like a plague of insects nibbling at
his mind, gnawing, biting, never letting him rest.

The white square. Where was it?
1:35.

The relay area. When?
1:40.

The rendezvous site. Please, please, please.
1:45.

At first they saw only the stegosaurs. Two of them.
The creatures sat in the middle of a wide clearing.
Their haunches squatted on the ground, their bony
backs jutting up like mountain ranges, their spiked
tails curled dangerously behind them.

He was almost ready to lead the party around them.
That would be the safest thing to do, considering the
fact that there wasn't much time left. He looked at his
watch. 1:50.

Something screamed danger in his mind. They had
tangled with stegosaurs once before, he knew. He
could not remember the exact incident. He only knew
that the stegosaurs had been dangerous.

He was about to turn away when he saw plainly the
area in which the stegosaurs were squatting. One of
the beasts raised its head, but Chuck wasn't looking at

that. He was looking at the creature's rump and at what the rump was partially covering.

A thick white line.

Realization came with a jolting shock!

The armor-plated dinosaurs were sitting in the relay area!

"Chuck, for the love of . . ."

"I know," Chuck shouted. He looked at his watch. 1:53.

"They're right inside the white square," Pete said. "What are we going to do?"

"I don't know." He gulped hard. "I . . . I don't know. We can't get inside it as long as they're in it."

"What time is it?" Dr. Perry asked.

Chuck looked at his watch again, noticing that his arm was trembling. "One fifty-four," he said.

"We must do something," Dr. Dumar offered. "We have only six minutes, haven't we?"

"Yes. Si-six minutes."

"I'll shoot them," Arthur said. "I've done enough hunting in my life. I should be able to get them both without much trouble."

Chuck shook his head. "Back-yard hunting isn't going to help with these monsters."

"Back yard?" Arthur looked surprised. "I've hunted in Africa, Chuck. I've killed rhinos and I can't see much difference here."

"Rhinos? Africa? You've . . ."

"What time is it?" Dr. Perry asked again.

"One fifty-five."

"Let me shoot them," Arthur said.

"No. We can't kill them inside the square. That'll

mean lugging them back to our own time. We can't do that. It's . . ."

"Never mind the law. So we can't bring back anything from the past. So what?" Pete's face flushed with anger.

"Let me try something else first," Chuck said. "If that doesn't work, we'll kill them on the spot. If we can."

"What do you want to try?"

"I'll try to get them out of the square. As soon as they're out, you folks run down there and get into it. Arthur, you can pick them off from the square. Then I'll get back and . . ."

"Suppose . . ."

"There isn't much time. I'm starting. Get down there as soon as they're out."

"Chuck . . ." Denise started, but he didn't wait for more. He sprinted across the clearing, coming closer to the huge, plated animals. He looked at his watch again. 1:57.

"Hoo-rah!" He shouted. "Hoorah! Hey, hey, hey!"

He began waving his arms wildly. The stegosaurs lifted their heads, stared at him stupidly. Without hesitation, Chuck unholstered his .45, released the safety and triggered off three fast shots.

The monsters lumbered to their feet.

"Come on!" Chuck bellowed. "Come on, you slow-witted idiots. Come on and get me!"

The beasts moved forward slowly, ponderously, still inside the square. Chuck fired again and again. Five shots. Two bullets left. And it was 1:58.

"Come on! Come on!"

And then they came. They came in a wild rush, a pair of Juggernauts that rumbled over the ground. Chuck began to run away from the stegosaurs, away from the white square of the relay area. From the corner of his eye he saw the party start across the clearing. He saw Arthur's rifle leave his shoulder, saw that the expedition was already within the square.

The beasts were close behind him, infuriated, tearing up the earth, ready to trample him to nothingness.

The first shot rang out. He heard a dull sound behind him, followed by an animal roar. He turned his head briefly. One of the dinosaurs was down, rolling over onto its side.

The other charged ahead furiously, anxious to get at its slippery quarry.

That was when Chuck tripped.

He fell to his knees, rolling over instantly. The beast was no more than five feet away. Chuck took a last look at his watch, brought up his .45 and fired two shots. The hammer clicked on an empty clip. There was no time to reload. A prayer began to form on his lips.

The second shot from Arthur thundered out in serious earnestness.

It caught the stegosaur at the back of his neck, and his head pitched forward. His snout hit the ground, plowing up earth a few feet from Chuck's face. The huge hulk seemed to shiver behind the head, quivering under the impact of the sudden stop. Before the beast rolled over, Chuck was on his feet and sprinting for the relay area.

"Hurry!" Arthur called.

He heard Denise moaning softly. "Chuck, Chuck, Chuck . . ."

His watch hands hovered between 1:59 and 2:00 P.M. A few seconds, just a few seconds.

"Chuck! Come on, boy!"

The ground seemed to slip by under his feet in a hazy blur. The white square was still so far away, so very far. And then the faces began to blur and the air began to shimmer around the square.

He ran and then dived, his arms outstretched. He hit the ground with a shock that sent the breath out of him.

Even as his mind told him that he had fallen short of the square, he felt a pair of powerful brown hands on his wrists, and he was being dragged violently across the ground, his skin scraping against the loose rocks and rough plants.

He tried to turn for a last look at the Jurassic. There was nothing to see any more. The land had been replaced by a flickering succession of colors and half-formed objects. He was safe within the square, and they were on their way home.

It seemed as if it had all never happened.

Here were his parents, his mother wet-eyed, his father proudly expanding his chest.

It had been just a routine return, until the authorities learned that Dr. Dumar and Dr. Perry had been found. The newspapers had been informed, then, and the TV newscasters.

The field was swarming with reporters now, flooded with TV trucks and commentators, microphones ex-

tended, cameras popping flash bulbs, excited crowds
shoving at the knot of returning hunters.

"Tell me, Mr. Baron," they asked, "are you glad you
financed the expedition?"

"I certainly am."

"You realize, of course, the importance of having
found the missing scientists?"

"I do. I've been on many an exciting hunt in my
lifetime—but this was the most exciting of all."

For a moment Chuck didn't know whom they were
addressing. He turned, a puzzled frown on his face.
The frown disappeared as he remembered who had
financed the expedition. Of course. How could he
have forgotten? Of course. The expedition had been
financed by . . .

"That, ladies and gentlemen," the newscaster said,
"was Mr. Arthur Baron, the millionaire big-game
hunter who financed this time slip to the Jurassic. Mr.
Baron, of course, needs no introduction. You will all
remember the spectacular headlines at the death of
J. D. Daniels, the multimillionaire sportsman. Mr.
Daniels left his entire fortune to be divided equally
between two men who had served him loyally for ten
years. One of these men was Arthur Baron."

Chuck smiled. Of course. Arthur. Of course.

"And now, ladies and gentlemen, a few words with
the lost scientists, Dr. Dumar and Dr. Perry. Tell me,
Dr. Perry, did you ever give up . . ."

The voices became a hum that swarmed around
Chuck. He listened, nodding his head, answering the
questions his parents put to him, feeling happy, warm.

Denise's parents were there, too—her mother a small

blonde woman with Denise's warm brown eyes and
pretty face. Her father was a tall, serious man, and he
took Chuck's hand gravely.

"Thank you, son," he said. "I was mighty worried
for a time."

"What do you think now, Denise?" her mother
asked.

"About what, mother?" Denise was smiling happily.

"Well, you insisted on permission to take a time slip.
You said you had to decide whether or not you wanted
to enter the special course for guides. You . . ."

"Nothing could change my mind now," Denise said.
"I love it." She took Chuck's hand and squeezed it
tightly. He looked down at her and grinned.

Of course! he thought. That was why Denise had
been along on the slip. The authorities had given her
special permission—they said that girl guides could be
as effective as men, and would certainly know how to
cope better with the female element. In fact, they had
encouraged Denise's presence, arguing that a girl in
the guide course would encourage other girls to enter.
He wondered why he was seemingly realizing all this
for the first time, but he shrugged his doubts aside.

"We will have to go back again," Dr. Dumar was
saying. "This time we'll pinpoint the deposit exactly,
and this time we'll return with a good map."

"Yes," Dr. Perry said. "And this time we'd like to
take a good guide with us from the beginning, so that
we won't get lost. A guide like Chuck Spencer."

Denise squeezed Chuck's hand again, and he felt
somehow proud, somehow more a man than he had a
little while ago.

"Thank you, Drs. Dumar and Perry," the newscaster was saying. "And now folks, the guide who brought the party back to civilization, the guide without whom the entire expedition would have failed—Chuck Spencer!"

There was applause. The crowd cheered. Slowly, his eyes filling with happy tears, Chuck stepped to the microphone.

ALEX
SCHOMBURG